The Final Rumble

By Rayven Skyy

DEDICATION

I dedicate The Final Rumble to my friend and Life Coach, Lovey Vawters. This past year has been a real rumble for the both of us and I think we have made it through the storm.

Acknowledgments

First and foremost I want to give God all honor, glory, and praise. He is truly my rock and without Him, none of this would be possible. I want to say thank you to my mommy, Janet Jordan who is still standing right behind me as she always have encouraging me to follow my dreams. I love you Ma!

I would like to thank Lovell Wilder Sr. for allowing me to borrow his face for the Rumble series. Lovelle, you have truly brought Milk's character to life!

To my editor Shannon Fields, The only word that comes to mind when I think of you is just AWESOME! I am so glad that I have found an editor that I gel with and who sees my visions when it comes to writing my books. I wish you all the success with impeccable Quality Editing You're one of the best out here and this is your year.

To Shantelle Brown . . . what would I do without you? I think you so much for supporting me when I first released A Rumble in VA. You are the best assistant that anyone could ask for and I wish you much continued success.

Proofreaders… Tasha Ringo, Kivi Cooper, Judy Frasier, Monica 'Moni' Craft and Shantelle Brown. Thanks once again ladies for all your hard work making sure The Final Rumble was perfect. Muah! {{{hugs}}} Singed copies of The Final Rumble will be sent out to you as soon as it is released in paperback.

Now to the readers . . . I have so many to name and if I missed you it was not on purpose. I have built genuine relationships with some of you because of Facebook and because you were fans of my books and I just want to acknowledge you! Nikki "Milkswife" Woodhouse a.k.a. Tonikia Trotter. You went really hard for me when you created that Facebook page dedicated to ARIVA and I really appreciate it. I hope you like the character I made in your honor in The Final Rumble. {{{hugs}}} I'kia Nicole, this is the reader that orders 4-6 books at a time to gift out to other people and she lives right here in VA! Thanks I'kia. I really appreciate your support. Marrisa Palmer, Sally McCargo, Stesha Manning (that's my girl right there) Arabia Dover, (Good luck with Coke Dreams) and I look forward to reading more of your books in the future. Anjela Day with a J, Malika Black Mclaughin, Detra Young, Camille Renee Lamb, Renee Brown-Fludd, Theresa Foggie, Karen Cummings, Farryn Grant and a host of others.

I want to give a very special shout out to Dionne Cross and Kesha Sutton-Henderson, my old Road Dawgs from Jr. High and High school. Thank you two so much for supporting me from day one. I still think of both of you when I hear *I Like*, by High-5. We may not talk every day or even every other day, but "true" and "real" friendship never dies. Bayside for life!

To all my family who continue to support me, thank you so much!

Rayven.

The Final Rumble

Study Long, Study Wrong!

I have always been a gambler and dice has always been my game of choice, but I had to fall back from playing years ago because I don't know when to stop.

I inherited my love of gambling from my grandma at a young age. I don't care what card game it was, you name it and Grandma knew how to play it. Granddad was always in the streets, and once my aunts and uncles moved out most of the time me and grandma were home alone. That was when she taught me how to play cards.

Every Thursday she would have a card game at our house with a group of ladies from the neighborhood. One night I asked her if I could play with them the next time they got together, but she told me no. Grandma said that I wasn't ready to play because I didn't know how to read the players. I didn't understand what she meant until I sat back one night and watched them play, but I wasn't only paying attention to how they played their hands. I was focused on their body language and then started to notice little things about each one of them.

When Ms. Ann had a good hand she would smile with her eyes, and when Ms. Dorothy's hand wont hitting on shit a crease formed in the corners

of her mouth. That's when I realized what grandma was talking about as far as reading the players.

I only spent a few months in Texas with my grandma. After, I left to Virginia where my cousin Kareem introduced me to the world of underground gambling. They called them Executive Games. To get into one of the gambling spots you had to know somebody that knew somebody and have at least a hundred grand to even get into the game.

The poker gods had been smiling down on me from the first time I played. I was on a serious winning streak until I hit a patch of bad luck, but when I found out Executive Games were being played in other states I moved around to see if my luck would change.

After shuffling, the dealer passed out the cards and placed the deck in the middle of the table. Now it was time to ante up. All of the players carefully placed an equal amount of money in the pot except me. I looked down at my cards and then around the table to see who I could read. Rich had on his usual poker face, but I could tell that Reid, the dude who was sitting across from me, ain't have shit by the way the muscles on his face flexed. I looked over at Lucy, the only female in the room, to find that she wasn't making eye contact with anyone, so I figured she was sitting on something.

"Chip in, Byrd! Ain't nobody got all night to wait on you," Rich said with frustration in his voice. "Man, you play like you taking a fucking test. This poker mothafucka', not algebra! Study long, study wrong."

I ignored his comments as I looked down at my hand once again and concluded it wasn't any good. Strong, but it wasn't a flush. Finally, I threw my bid in, and since I was the player at the immediate left of the dealer it was on me.

"Check," I sternly said, passing the decision to Lucy.

"See," Lucy responded just as sternly, matching the amount of the pot.

"I fold," Reid said, placing his cards face down on the table. I was right, he didn't have shit.

"I raise this mothafucka," Rich confidently said, tossing in some chips. "Do you want me to play your hand for you, nigga?"

"Man, shut the fu-" I was about to throw my bid in when the door of the room was kicked in. One by one people dressed in all black with full faced scullys entered the room brandishing guns.

"If you don't want to die tonight get yo' mothafuckin' ass down on the floor!" one of the masked men hollered.

Since dying today was not on my list of things to do, I did what he said along with everybody else. Even Rich's shit talking ass wasted no time in getting down on the floor.

"You . . . and you," the masked man said between clenched teeth, pointing to the men who were acting as our security guards, "get up against the wall!"

They both turned around at the same time and put their hands up. The masked man nodded to one of the other dudes who had charged in the room behind him.

"Check them 'cause I know they strapped," he said, referring to their guns. I slowly scanned the room with my eyes without being obvious, or so I thought. "Turn yo' mothafuckin' head the other way, nigga!" He quickly pointed his gun in my face.

"A'ight, man, a'ight," I turned my head the other way to show him that I didn't want no trouble.

"Now, this is how this shit is gon' go down," he said, taking his focus off of me. "When I tell you to, stand up and empty out yo' pockets. One false move, and next week you'll be taking a dirt nap after one of yo' family members identifies the body."

Now that I was facing the other way I was looking directly at Lucy. The masked man walked over to the other side of the room and Lucy was slowly moving her hand down the side of her leg as if she was reaching for something. She had on boots that came up to her thighs where she could easily conceal a weapon.

"Yo' turn mothafucka'," I heard the robber say.

Lucy now had something in her hand that she was slowly raising up from the inside of her boot. We stared at each other for a minute and used our eyes to talk, and I thought we were both speaking the same language. I had my gun tucked in the small of my back, but as soon as I reached for it Lucy pulled out her gun and pointed it at me.

"Really?" she questioned, cocking the gun. "Who the fuck is you supposed to be, Robin Hood? Drop it!" She motioned with her gun. I put my gun down on the floor beside me and Lucy stood up over top of me. "Stand up on your feet Byrd 'cause I want to personally be the one to take yo' shit. As much money I have lost to you . . ." I stood up. "I've been looking at that pinky ring on your finger all night, nigga. Let me get that. I glanced down at the ring that once belonged to my granddad, slid it off my finger, and handed it to her. "Is there a problem?" Lucy tilted her head to the side. "You mad?"

"Fuck you! I'll get it back." I sucked my teeth and she smacked me in my face.

"Shut up! You talk, too, damn much." Lucy put the gun up to my forehead and started ravaging my pockets. "I see we came prepared tonight," she said with a smirk, flashing my own money up to my face. "I guess you will get this back, too, huh?" Lucy smiled. "Give me one of those duffle bags," she said to no one in particular. "Get back down on the ground." She nodded at me with her head and then slapped me across my face again. "Hurry up, you taking too long. I ain't got all night!"

The View!

Of all the chairs in this room, I had to sit by the raunchiest smelling bitch in here. She literally smells like something crawled up her ass and died. My momma always told me if you can smell yourself somebody else can smell you, too, and this bitch smells like a barrel of funk. I should've known something was up when the two girls that were sitting beside her before we broke for lunch were now sitting on the other side of the room. I glanced at her papers and saw that her name was Tanisha. If you ask me, her momma should have named her Fish n' Chips.

"Now, if your interview is scheduled for nine o'clock you may want to arrive at least fifteen to twenty minutes early. This shows your potential employer that you are serious about obtaining the job and if hired you will be punctual."

I looked around the room as I tuned Jackie, the coordinator of 'The View', out. I couldn't believe the way some of these women left the house this morning. I know this is social services, but damn!

"I have a question," Tanisha stated, raising her hand.

"Feel free to ask any questions you may have," Jackie happily replied.

"What if suntin' happens and it makes you late for the job interview?" Tanisha asked, while rolling her neck.

"What if what happens?" Jackie looked at Tanisha with a confused look on her face.

"What if suntin' happens," Tanisha repeated, wearing a very serious expression on her face.

"*Suntin'*?" Jackie looked around the room as if she was waiting for somebody to translate what Tanisha just said. Apparently she didn't speak Ebonics. I was trying my best to hold in my laughter.

"Yeah, what if suntin' happens to make you late for the interview?" Tanisha said, with an increasing attitude.

"Oh, you mean something?" Jackie confidently questioned with a sigh of relief, now that she was able to decipher what Tanisha was saying.

"That's what I said. Suntin'," Tanisha rolled her eyes and pressed her lips together. "I have four kids and suntin' could happen to make me late."

I looked up at the water stained tiles on the ceiling and thought, '*If this bitch says "suntin'" one more time I'm going to knock her stinkin' ass out the chair!*'

"Well, in the event that something unforeseen was to happen you should contact the person who scheduled the interview with you to see if you could possibly reschedule for a later time. But, I have to be honest with you. Most likely you will not get the job," Jackie answered.

 Rayven Skyy

Tanisha started to speak as a chill went up my spine, "Dat ain't right! What if suntin' happens to make 'dem late? Shit happens!" I closed my eyes and took a deep breath. Come on four o'clock so I can get away from this tangy, no talking ass bitch. I'm ready to go pick up my baby Saysha and go home.

"You're right, but you are trying to get the job. Not the other way around. Alright," Jackie quickly said, switching the subject before Fish n' Chips could come back with a rebuttal, "I'm going to let you go a little early today because I have a staff meeting to attend." 'Hallelujah,' I thought. "Make sure you are on time tomorrow morning." She looked directly at Tanisha. "We will start promptly at eight. Enjoy the rest of your day."

I put my purse on my shoulder, got up, and was at the elevator doors before God got the news. I was trying to beat Tanisha there so I wouldn't have to smell her ass on the way downstairs, but she was in as much of a hurry to leave as everyone else and beat me to the elevator door. Being that was the case; I decided to take the stairs.

By the time I made it down and outside to the bus stop, Tanisha was already there sitting down on the bench smoking a Black and Mild cigar. Some of the other girls that were in 'The View' class were there, too, but they were all standing up even though there was plenty of room for them to sit down. I assumed they all knew that Tanisha was allergic to water and that was the reason they were

8

all still standing up. I can't say I blame them. If it meant sitting next to Tanisha again, I'll stand up and wait for the bus, too.

I looked at my cell phone to see what time it was. Shit, only three fifteen. The Virginia Beach 20 bus didn't come again for another fifteen minutes. I looked around to see if there was a store nearby that I could go browsing in to kill some time even though I didn't have any money to spend. When I turned back around, there was a gold BMW that had stopped at the light in front of the bus stop. I shook my head and thought, *'Of all the damn days.'*

"You need a ride, Sabrina?"

"Bitch fuck you!" I said to Nicole.

"Are you sure? It's awful hot out here today," she asked in a condescending tone. "Really, I don't mind."

"Kiss my ass!" I told her, looking the other way.

Nicole started laughing. "That I don't do, but you on the other hand have kissed mine several times. You know our baby daddy is an ass man. How did it taste?"

"I wrote the book on him kissing my ass bitch, so you tell me how my ass tastes," I snapped back, ignoring the fact that the people at the bus stop may have been paying attention to us. I didn't care.

"Whatever, bitch! You should have called me if you needed some money. I don't mind helping you out. After all, our kids are siblings. You didn't have to come down here and beg these white folks for that little bit of money and food stamps."

I dropped my pocketbook on the ground along with the papers I had in my hand and walked towards Nicole's car, but the light turned green and she sped off. *'That's alright,'* I thought to myself, *'I got something up the road for that bitch!'*

***

Singing . . .

"Lovers come . . . and then lovers go . . . that's what folks say . . . don't they know . . . they're not there when you love me, hold me, and say you care . . . and what we have is much more than they can see. . . "

I took off my headphones when I saw Juju standing in the doorway of my bedroom. I closed up my wedding album and sat it down on the nightstand next to my bed. I quickly wiped my eyes so he wouldn't see that I had been crying. I know that I am living in his house but damn, whatever happened to knocking?

"Whatchu' in here doing, bitch?" he said, sauntering into the room.

"Shhh . . ." I put my index finger up to my lips. "Please don't wake her up, Juju," I pleaded, looking over at Saysha. I slowly got up off the bed; tip toed out of the room, and closed the bedroom door behind me. Then I walked into the living room. "What's up?" I asked, sitting down on the couch.

"I was just checkin' on you. You stay cooped up in that room so much being antisocial. I just wanted to make sure you didn't hang yourself in the closet. And why are your eyes so swollen?"

"Allergies," I quickly responded, lying through my teeth.

"Allergies my ass! Bitch, I know crying eyes when I see it," Juju snapped. "Sabrina, Sabrina," he sighed while shaking his head, "What iz' I gon' do with you?" Juju put his right hand on his hips.

"What do you mean, 'what are you going to do with me?' " I pressed my lips together and looked at him frankly.

"Oh, bitch, don't get no attitude!" Juju rolled his neck at me. "That's all you do is sit in this house, mope, and listen to sad love songs. Milk is in jail, not you!"

"Am I bothering you?" I snapped back, becoming frustrated by the conversation.

"Yes, bitch, you are!" Juju now had both hands on his hips. "You're fuckin' up the aurora in this mothafucka'." Juju waved his arms in the air signaling the entire house.

"Do you want me to leave your house, Juju? Is that what you are trying to say?" I stood up and got very defensive.

"Sabrina, that's not what I am saying. Don't you dare try and carry me like that! That would be a jealous bitch move and you know I don't get down like that!" Juju pointed directly at me obviously upset that I would approach him like that. "You

know that you can stay here for as long as you need to." He took a deep breath and calmed down some. "I just don't like to see you like this," Juju sincerely stated, shaking his head at me and taking his hands off of his hips.

"Like what?" I raised my voice, throwing my hands up in the air.

"Wait a minute, wait a minute! All that feisty shit is so unnecessary," he said. "I know you miss your man and all that, but trust me when I tell you that he would not be sitting around no damn house strumming his pain with his fingers if it were yo' ass sitting in Alcatraz!" I put my hands down and turned my head the other way so that Juju would not see me laughing. "What the hell is so funny, bitch? I'm serious. . ."

"Your ass is what's funny." I laughed. "Alcatraz, Juju? For real?"

"Hell, Alcatraz, Sing Sing . . ." He waved his hands around. "Pelican Bay . . . they're all the same. Prison is prison." He popped his lips. I sat back down on the couch and Juju sat down beside me. "The moral of my story is this . . . sometimes you have to just roll with it when your life is interrupted, baby. You ever heard that Steve Windward song . . . *'You just roll with it baby. . .'*?" Juju started singing and snapping his fingers. "*Roll with it baby. . .*"

"Okay, yes I know the song." I grabbed Juju's hands with mine so that he would stop singing. "I get it!"

"Well, good then. I'mma' need you to just roll with it. Your chocolate Boo Thang' will be home soon enough, so take this time and focus on you. You are too dependent on Milk, and right now Milk can't do anything for you . . . I don't mean that in a bad way."

"I know you don't and I'm sorry for yelling at you. I just miss him so much," I responded, starting to get emotional again.

"I'm sure you do," he nodded his head in agreement, "but in the meantime . . . tomorrow let's go get manis and pedis."

"Juju, you know I don't have any money," I said, looking down at the sofa cushion with shame.

"I know you don't witcha' po' ass," Juju batted his eyelashes at me. He is the only person that could have said that without me going off. "It's my treat."

"You don't have to do that, Juju. You have done more than enough just by letting me and Saysha stay here."

"I know I don't have to do nothing but stay gorgeous and die, and I plan on doing that, too, but look how many times you have treated me. And besides, I don't want you to turn into a jealous bitch 'cause I keep my nails and toes done." He started laughing. "And speaking of jealous bitches," he slapped his hand on his thigh, "Milk's baby momma gets this week's jealous bitch award."

"Umph . . . that's the last person I want to talk about. I saw her ass today," I said, referring to

Nicole. Juju was now working at the same shop as Nicole. Once Milk went to prison she must've not been able to afford to keep her shop open. Not too long after she had Mj she closed the salon and is now doing hair at Cut N' Curl again. "What did she do?" Curiosity got the best of me.

"That bitch stole some of my hair products!"

"Stole them?" I made a confused face as I looked at Juju. "Why would she steal your stuff and how do you know it was her?" I asked.

"Cause my shit mysteriously started to grow legs when she came back to work at Cut N' Curl with her trifling ass. It takes Angelle to tell you 'bout that bitch." Angelle was another stylist who worked in the shop with them.

"Why you say that, Juju?"

"Well, you know Angelle's cousin runs a twenty-four hour daycare and she keeps your stepson." I popped Juju on his arm. "Owww..."

"He is not my damn stepson." I laughed because I knew he was trying to be funny.

"Well, Saysha's little brother then." He put his hands up to block mine. "Bitch, if you don't stop hitting me!" He then started laughing, too.

"Just get on with what you were going to tell me."

"Anyway . . . Angelle told me that her cousin said Nicole leaves that po' chile' at that damn daycare all day and don't go pick him up until eleven o'clock at night, sometimes longer. They say the baby always smells like sour milk and looks like he don't belong to nobody."

"What?" My eyes popped wide open as I listened to Juju.

"Ain't it sad? That bitch walk around looking like she just stepped off a runway in Milan and the baby looking like he should be in an infomercial for Feed the Chirren'."

"That's fucked up, and I'm damn sure going to tell Milk."

"For what," Juju looked at me. "What can he do?"

"Yeah, I guess you're right. Well, I ain't got nothing to do with it anyway." I stood up. "That's between her and Milk. I'm getting ready to go take me a shower."

"I'mma' tell you what you need to do and that's come up to the shop and let me touch that kitchen back there up!" Juju put his index finger on the nape of his neck to indicate where he was talking about on my neck. "What I tell you 'bout walking 'round here looking wretched!" He pressed his lips together again and made a sour face. "The only people who can get away with nappy roots is the rap group *Nappy Roots*." He shook his head in disdain.

"Shut up," I shouted, swatting at him. "I know I need to get my hair done, but coming up to Cut N' Curl is not an option for me now that Nicole works there. I don't want to see that bitch! Why you can't do my hair here at the house like you've been doing?"

"Cause I don't have most of my supplies here and fuck that jealous bitch! Nicole talks a lot of shit, but she don't want none of you for real."

Last Lick!

"Put it all in me Byrd and stop teasing me," Lucy begged, digging in my back with her manicured nails.

"Get it how you want it." I had my hands gripped tightly around her ankles and her legs spread apart wide. I was going to make her work for this dick tonight. Lucy reached up, put her hands firmly on my ass, and then pulled me towards her causing me to lose my balance.

"I want it all!" she growled.

By the hold Lucy had on my dick with her pussy, I could tell she did kegal exercises on the regular. I may have been on top but Lucy was the one doing all of the work. The way she was throwing the pussy to me you would think that she was the one with the dick. I almost gave in and allowed her to have her way with me, but fuck that. I work pussy, pussy don't work me. I put both of Lucy's legs in the folds of my arms and lifted her up.

"You trying your best to take it all ain't you?" I questioned, with cockiness.

"Who better than me," she answered in between her panting. I pinned Lucy up against the wall and put my hand around her neck. "Do it," she commanded.

"Do what?" I already knew what she wanted, but I was going to make her beg for it.

"Choke me," she whispered. I tightened my hand around her neck. "Harder!" she yelled.

"I should choke the shit out of you for the way you slapped me in my face the other night," I said, thrusting my dick so far inside that I could feel her heartbeat on the tip. "Say please!" I gripped a handful of her hair and pulled on it with my other hand.

"Please . . . uhh . . . please." Lucy was into all that S&M shit. Not only did she want to be fucked, but she wanted to get fucked up. Literally! "Harder!" I applied some more pressure around her neck and went into beat it up mode. She broke the grip I had on her legs and wrapped them around my waist.

"Don't forget who the real boss is. You ain't running shit for real, and where the fuck is my Granddad's ring?"

I commenced to fucking the shit out of her and opted to take a shower once I got home instead of in the hotel room we were in. I gave Lucy her share of the money from the robbery and left. I know I have some explaining to do, so let me start from when I left Texas.

The streets of Miami were in disarray when I returned after my hiatus. I was all prepared to go to war with Gremlin to reclaim what was mine up until I ran into Smurf, a nigga that grew up with me and Gremlin out in Pork n' Beans. He told me he had not seen or heard from Gremlin. When Smurf told me that he heard he was ganked out of 100k for some powdered milk instead of dope, I knew exactly who was behind it, Milk, and I took that shit personally.

Not because of Gremlin, I could give a fuck about him. I'm sure he is burning in hell right now compliments of Milk. He must have figured out the same way I did that Gremlin was the one who put everything in motion for us to battle it out in the streets, but to know that he could stretch his arm all the way down to Florida to get at the nigga undetected rubbed me the wrong way. Milk was a nine lives having ass mothafucka', and if he could get at Gremlin like he did then he could do the same thing to me.

I had fucked up most of my money gambling so I came home to get it back up. I lost touch with Chino, my old connect and finding the good raw was becoming too much work. I needed a good lick that was going to pay off, so instead of robbing niggas in the street I started hitting up the executive games and this last lick put me right where I needed to be. Now, I'm ready to take me a road trip.

 Rayven Skyy

Trust!

"Milk?"

"What's up?" I turned around in the chair.

"He just called yo' name man," Pound, my cell mate, answered.

"Oh shit. Thanks man."

I got up and walked towards the CO who was passing out the mail. After he handed mine to me, I looked down at the envelopes to see who they were from. There was a letter from Sabrina and one from her niece, Ladybug. I went back to the pod that I shared with Pound so that I could have some privacy and opened Sabrina's letter first.

"Milk,

Let me first start off by saying that I love you, I miss you, and I am counting down the days until you come home. Juju is going to let me use his car so I will be able to visit you this weekend. Your daughter needs to spend some time with her daddy. I ended up having to take the picture of you two off the dresser because every time she looked at it she started crying.

I finally swallowed my pride and went down to Social Services and applied for food stamps. I also qualified for Medicaid and TANF, but in order to get the TANF check I had to enroll myself into a Workforce program called 'The View' which I am really not feeling at all. But I have to do what I have to do.

I'm not trying to start anything, but I feel as if I need to tell you this since it is concerning your son. I don't know if you know this or not but Juju works in the same hair salon as Nicole, so you won't have to wonder who told me this, and from what he tells me Nicole is not taking care of Mj like she should be. I've seen Nicole on several occasions, and I know how she carries herself, so there is no excuse for the baby to be looking like he does. I don't want you to think the only reason why I am bringing this to your attention is because I can't stand the bitch, because I think you already know how I feel about her, but I am thinking in the best interest of your child.

Sorry this letter is so short but I have to get up early in the morning for that bullshit ass class. I just wanted to drop you a few lines before I went to bed. I love you always and forever.

Sabrina."

I read Sabrina's letter one more time before I folded it up and put it back in the envelope. Then I got up, left out of my pod, and walked back down to the dayroom. The line for the phone was long, so I sat down at an empty table to wait. You already know who I'm calling, but while I'm waiting

 Rayven Skyy

for the phone why don't you pull up a seat and let me bring you up to speed with what's been going on since we last spoke. You better pay attention because it's a lot. Shit, I don't even know where to begin.

Being in the game as long as I have I would be a fool to think that I was untouchable. Every dog has its day and that goes for hustlers, too. There are certain things you must have in place just in case you're faced with a setback, whether it be getting robbed, killed, or tore off by the police. The only thing that saved me from a twenty-five to forty year sentence was the fact that I had anonymously made contributions to city officials on the barbershop's behalf.

I even took it to the state level and made campaign contributions to the Governors since Mark Warner was in office. Picture those headlines. Not to mention the fact that some of the alleged snitchers were suddenly starting to have a change of heart not long after Maine and Lee started paying a few family members visits. They hurried up and dropped them charges against me. I did take a plea for the gun they found in the house and was sentenced to five years with four years suspended.

One thing you have to do when you are in the game is take care of your lawyer and I don't mean only when you get in trouble. Give him ten percent of everything as you make it and he will fight to the end for your freedom. He can't get paid with you sitting in jail. The money he gets from you is what's paying for his family vacations and if you can find one that will accept some dope for services rendered you really good, but old Uncle Sam was not letting me off the hook that easily.

Once Sabrina was released she wasn't allowed to go back to the house because the IRS seized everything. Everything of value down to the mothafuckin' clothes were liquidated and the money was applied to the taxes we owed, along with every dollar I had in the business and personal accounts. That's when I found out that Sabrina had a bank account and credit cards of her own that I didn't know about, but not anymore.

After the shooting at her momma's house, Ms. Janis said that she didn't feel comfortable living there by herself so she moved into a one bedroom apartment uptown. There wasn't enough room for Sabrina and the baby to move in with her so she ended up moving in with her cousin, Juju. I asked Sabrina why she didn't just ask her sister, Stephanie, if she could stay with her until I came home, but Sabrina said she would eat her own toenails before she asked her sister to do anything for her.

The only money I had left to my name was the 100k I beat Gremlin for, plus another fifty grand Dap was holding for me. I told him how much money to give Sabrina and Nicole each month so they would be alright until I came home, but I guess Dap had other plans for my money. He did put a thousand dollars on my canteen once I went to prison. He must have felt that was the least he could do, but that shit hurt me. Dap was like a

father to me and I had much respect for him, but what are you gonna' do?

Nicole went back to work at Lea's shop a couple of months after she had the baby. I wasn't too thrilled about my son being kept by strangers, but there was really no choice in the matter. I don't have any family that could keep him and the last thing I was going to do was fix my lips to ask Sabrina to babysit Mj while Nicole worked.

"Are you waiting on the phone man?" Pound sat down at the table.

"Yeah man," I answered him, without looking in his direction. My eyes were now fixated on the woman walking around with one of the correctional officers.

"Got damn," Pound said aloud. "I know her legs are tired from holding up all that ass." Sgt. Trotter was the dorm supervisor and she didn't take no shit. "Man, I'm going to take me a shower. My dick getting hard just looking at her with her mean ass."

I got up when I saw the dude that was on the phone hang up the receiver and walked over to the phones that were lined up on the wall. I quickly dialed Nicole's number.

"This is ITI. You have a collect call from. . ."

"Milk," I stated my name when prompted.

"This call is from an inmate in the Greensville Federal Correctional Center. You have a limited amount of calls left before service will be interrupted. To make billing arrangements please visit us on the web at www.offenderconnect.com.

To accept this call press one. To refuse this call and block any future calls from this facility press nine or simply hang up." I waited until our call was connected.

"Yo," I angrily shouted.

"Hey," Nicole answered calmly.

"Ain't no mothafuckin' 'hey'," I yelled into the phone. "What the fuck is going on with my son?"

Something to Talk About!

When I found out that I was pregnant I was fit to be tied. Y'all know I don't do kids. Luckily for me he wasn't a hollering ass baby. In fact, he hardly ever cries and that's my kind of baby. I do all the things that the law requires me to do and that's keep a roof over his head, food in his stomach, and clothes on his back, which mostly come from Wal-Mart. I put the good clothes on him when I take him to go see Milk, but it's not written anywhere that I have to hold him or even rock him to sleep. I'm just holding on until his pappy is released. Then he can go live with Milk and Sabrina and they can all be one big, happy family. I have no problem with signing over my rights to his father just like I did with Bre.

Milk walked into the visitor's room looking around and I know he was expecting to see Sabrina. I waved my hand in the air to get his attention, and he started walking towards the table where I was sitting at holding Mj.

"Whatchu' doing here Nicole," he asked. All of the inmates had to sit facing the guards and after he sat down in his assigned seat he took Mj out of my arms.

"What do you mean what am I doing here? I told you on the phone the last time I talked to you that I was coming up here on Friday." I lied.

"No you didn't. . ." He shook his head at me. "You know that it was Sabrina's week to come see me." He looked down at Mj. "What's going on, man?" He turned Mj around to face him. "You getting big as shit." Milk held him up and then sat him back down in his lap.

"Oh, I must have gotten the weeks mixed up." I lied again.

"I know I'mma' hear 'bout this shit tomorrow," Milk said, never taking his attention away from Mj.

The prison didn't allow the inmates to use the phones on Fridays, that's why I picked today to come see Milk. By the time they turn the phones on in the morning Sabrina will already be on her way up here to see him. I know ain't nobody tell Milk all that bullshit but Sabrina, and I'm sure it was told to her by her cousin RuPaul, meaning Juju. Milk is right. He is going to hear about this shit later, and I'm going to give the bitch something to talk about!

For Old and New!

As I was walking up the sidewalk to Cut N' Curl I saw Juju standing outside smoking a cigarette. When he realized it was me walking towards him he started waving his hand at me like he was in a Miss America pageant.

"I'm oh so glad you decided to come up here and let me do something to that wig, but you should have called me first. I got two under the dryer now." Juju dropped his cigarette butt on the ground and stepped on it with his three hundred dollar Gucci loafer. I stormed right past him without saying anything.

I flung the shop doors open with Juju right behind me and looked around the salon. Nicole and I locked eyes on each other at the same time. One thing I don't do is talk shit with bitches. If I'm going to do something to you there ain't nothing to have a conversation about, and by the stance she was in I could tell Nicole was a woman of few words, too. She knew what I came there for, so without further ado I charged towards her station. The girl who was sitting in her chair getting her hair done got up just as my fist connected with Nicole's chin. I was going to beat this bitch's ass for old and new.

Nicole countered my punch with one of her own, but that was the last lick she was able to get in before she hit the ground. The salon chair was knocked over along with half of the hair products on her station. We rolled on top of each other until I pinned Nicole down on the floor, and that was all she wrote. Juju, who doesn't weigh a hundred pounds soaked and wet, tried to pull me off to no avail. I had a lot of pent up rage inside of me and I was taking it all out on Nicole's face.

Lea, the shop owner, was able to help Juju pull me off of her and Janea, another bitch I can't stand, grabbed Nicole from behind once she got up off the floor. It took both Juju and Lea to drag me outside but I could still see Nicole through the window. She was doing a lot of hand motioning to me, but she did not once walk towards that door to come outside and greet me again.

"I cannot believe you at my job acting a fool," Juju frantically said, out of breath. I know trying to get control of me was a real work out for him. "Got my brand new shoes all trampled on and scuffed up. Shit!" He looked down at his shoes.

"Leave me alone right now, Juju," I said, turning around to walk away.

"Uh . . . uhh!" Juju followed behind me. "What the fuck did the jealous bitch do?"

"She knows what she did," I said, and kept walking.

I was almost at the prison when Milk called my cell phone and told me that Nicole came up there to visit him the day before. I didn't say anything to him; I just hung up the phone. I called my niece Aleeaha and asked her if she would watch Saysha for an hour for me, and as soon as I dropped her off at my sister's house I was on my mission. Just like that.

After I left Cut N' Curl, I went right back to my Stephanie's house to pick up Saysha like nothing happened. I didn't want her to stay there too long because sometimes Stephanie acts like she has a problem with Aleeaha watching my baby, but by the time I got back to her house she still wasn't home. My momma was there though. She told me that Saysha was running a slight fever, so once I got her home, bathed, and fed I gave her some Children's Tylenol. She has been asleep ever since.

After I hung up on Milk earlier he tried calling me back but I didn't answer the phone. After his third attempt he didn't call back until now. I answered my cell phone and listened to the recording until it prompted me to press one.

"Hey, Bae," Milk said.

"Hello," I replied.

"What's wrong?"

"Nothing." I wanted to scream, '*You know what the fuck is wrong with me*,' but I didn't.

"Don't tell me that Sabrina. I can hear it all in your voice. Where my baby at?" he questioned.

"She's asleep."

"Wake her up so I can talk to her."

"No. She has a fever so I gave her some medicine and she just went to sleep," I said with an attitude.

"Sabrina, I'mma' ask you one more time. What's wrong with you?"

"Nothing, Milk," I said, raising my voice.

"You keep saying nothing but you sound like you got something on yo mind. Go 'head and speak yo peace. We already done wasted five minutes of this twenty minute phone call." I didn't say anything. "Look, Sabrina, I told you the girl said she got the weekends mixed up. . ."

"Bullshit!" I was now yelling. "That bitch ain't get shit mixed up. She knew it was my weekend to come and see you. Her trifling ass did that shit on purpose and I'm tired of you always taking up for the shit she do."

"What was I supposed to do Sabrina, refuse the visit?"

"You got damn right!" I continued to yell.

"Bae, come on. . ."

"No, Milk, I'm sick of her ass. Why does she have to come up there anyway? I can bring Mj with me when I come to see you."

"I already asked her to do that and she said no. I told you that," Milk responded.

"I don't see why the fuck not. As long as you get to see your son what does it matter?"

"Would you let her bring Saysha up here?" I didn't answer him because he already knew the

answer. "And you ain't have to go up to the shop and do what you did either."

"Oh, so you and that bitch must really talk on the regular. She just saw you yesterday so I don't see what y'all have so much to talk about. While she was reporting to you like you are the police, did the bitch tell you I put her BMW on kickstands, too?" I asked, referring to the tires I slashed on Nicole's car before I went inside the shop.

"Yeah she did, and she said she gon' put a warrant out on yo' ass for that shit, too."

"And I'mma' beat her ass again!"

"Lord, Jesus, keep me near the cross," Milk said, lowering his voice and sighing.

"That bitch has really got you fooled don't she?" I let out a slight chuckle.

"Got me fooled how, Sabrina?" He was the one who was yelling now

"You think she's coming up there just so you can see that baby. Nicole don't give a fuck about her child for real. Not the way that I heard she keeps him."

"He always straight when she brings him up here to see me," Milk said, defending Nicole.

"That's because she knows better and that's what I'm talking about right there. What I tell you don't mean shit. You act like that bitch can't do no wrong," I shot back at Milk, getting more of an attitude.

"Sabrina, what the fuck you want me to do? I'm in mothafuckin' prison! What can I do with her ass while I'm in here?" he hollered through the phone. "I don't fuck with Nicole like that no more. How many times do I have to tell you that?"

"Milk, I don't even want to talk about it anymore," I said, trying to release the aggravation. "I ain't got nothing else to say about your baby momma."

"Sabrina, whatchu' want me to do?" he calmly asked. "My son is here and she can't push him back up."

"I said I'm through talking about it. . ."

"A'ight then, fuck it!"

"Is there a problem?" I asked, cocking my head to the side as if Milk could see me.

"Yeah, it's a mothafuckin' problem. You and Nicole ain't got to like each other, but got damn! Y'all can't try to get along for the kid's sake? I feel like a mothafuckin' referee," Milk was now yelling again.

"Your call will be disconnected in three minutes."

"You see what I mean. The mothafuckin' call almost over and once again we talkin' 'bout the same bullshit!"

"Milk, just call back."

"Man, naw . . . I ain't calling back tonight, Sabrina. Kiss my baby for me."

"Your call will be disconnected in two minutes."

"Milk. . ."

"I'm not calling back tonight, Sabrina. Y'all 'bout to stress me the fuck out. I can't fight you and

these mothafuckin' bars, too!"

"Your call will be disconnected in one minute."

"Are you going to call me tomorrow?" I asked.

"Naw . . . I probably won't call 'til next week."

"I love you," I said. Even though I was mad we always told each other that we loved one another before the phone would hang up. When Milk didn't respond I told him that I loved him again in case he didn't hear me the first time, which I know he did.

"Love you, too," he said, before hanging up.

Knock, knock. I turned around and it was Juju. "Well how are we doing Leila Ali?" he asked attempting to be funny. "Scoot over," Juju said, sitting down. "Sabrina, you ain't have to beat the jealous bitch's ass like you did. She got a lump so big on her forehead that the bitch look like the boy from the movie, *The Mask.*" Juju started fanning himself as he laughed hysterically. "Bitch, why you ain't turn the air on when you came home? It's hot as goose grease in here."

Juju told me that the police came up to Cut N' Curl after I left. Nicole wasn't lying when she told Milk that she was going to put a warrant out on me for assault. She even got a restraining order against me. I went and turned myself in the next day and after four hours I was released on a PR bond. When Milk called me later on during the week, he didn't say anything else about my fight with Nicole and neither did I. Nicole and I have to go to court on Friday. Pray for me y'all.

Bum Bitch Status!

I ended up dropping the charges I put out on Sabrina when I realized I was acting off my emotions, which is something that I never do. I lost focus of the real task at hand and that was operation 'get rid of Mj'. I even asked Milk to give me Sabrina's cell phone number so I could call her myself to squash our beef and told him I would try my best to get along with his girlfriend.

He didn't give me her number of course, but I didn't want the bitch's number for real anyway. I just wanted to appear to Milk as the peace maker. Breon just had a daughter when he and I first got together, so I know how to deal with baby mommas and girlfriends. I don't know why women who have a baby by a man first act like their child takes precedence over any kids that are born after. What makes their child the most important? They're all his damn kids!

Ladies, when you run across baby mommas like these kill those bitches with kindness in a nice but nasty way. Don't ever be the one to start the fights and your baby daddy will always take your side because you don't come off as the one who is always starting shit. That is the one thing I lost sight of.

Also, remember to always look your very best when you know that you will be coming in contact with her. She will be so worried and stressed out about whether you are still fucking with him or not and will eventually end up letting herself go. The man you two may have shared at one time really ain't going to want her ass then. She will instantly become as Juju would say, "a jealous bitch!" Speaking of sweetness, ever since he has been out of town the shop has been more peaceful. I don't know who talks about dick more, Juju or Janea.

Oh, and I hear Sabrina is well on her way to official bum bitch status. Well, I actually overheard a client tell Janea that she saw Sabrina in the rental office somewhere in Virginia Beach putting in an application for public housing. I can't wait to drop Mj off to his daddy when he comes home just to rub her face in the fact that her living quarters have been reduced to the size of a doll house. I know Milk will be living there, too.

How do you be with a mothafucka in the game for years and not have your own bama with all the access she had to Milk's money? Such foolishness. Fuck love, pay me!

What's in it for Me!

"Who is it?"

"Is Yvette home?" I responded. Even I didn't recognize the voice, and when the voice didn't respond I knocked on the door again. I stood there and waited for at least two minutes before the door finally opened, and when it did I was able to see who the voice belonged to. "Is Yvette here?"

"Who are you?" she asked.

"A friend," I answered. "Now, is she here?" The white girl stared blankly at me as if she was in a daze. I could tell just by looking at her that she was dusty.

"Hold on a second," she said, shutting the door in my face.

I zipped the North Face jacket I was wearing all the way up and rubbed my hands together. I've been back in Virginia for a few days and still haven't adjusted to the cold weather. When the door opened again I had to do a double take.

"Are you kidding me?" Yvette said, stepping outside onto the porch and closing the door behind her. "What the hell do you want, Rico?"

"Yvette?" I asked in disbelief.

"Look, Sabrina ain't here," she said, turning around to walk back into the house.

Rayven Skyy

"Wait a minute, Yvette." I put my hand on her shoulder. "Let me talk to you for a second." Yvette jumped and quickly turned around.

"Don't put your damn hands on me," she yelled.

"Okay, okay!" I could see that I scared her by the way she flinched, but I could also tell that she was high, too. "I'm not going to hurt you, Yvette. I just really need to get in touch with Sabrina." I slowly took a step back. "Calm down. . ." I put my hands up.

"Get in touch with Sabrina for what? That is not your baby, Rico, so I don't know why you even came back to Virginia." Yvette rolled her eyes at me.

Sabrina must not have told her that she saw me when I got out of jail and right before I left for Texas. "Look, Yvette, I really need to speak to Sabrina."

"What's in it for me?" Yvette cunningly asked, putting her hands on her hips.

"A whole lot can be in it for you," I casually responded.

When Yvette opened the door and told me I could come inside I knew then that it would be only a matter of time before I was face to face with Sabrina again.

Rolling in the Deep!

Thank God today is Friday and I don't have to go back to the Workforce class until Monday. I have just enough time to take a shower and cook dinner before my momma drops Saysha off to me.

I stepped off of the bus and waited for it to drive off before I crossed the street. As I walked towards the apartment, I noticed a silver Infinity with tinted windows parked by the dumpster that was still running. It had rims on it too but I couldn't tell you what brand they were. It must belong to someone who just moved into the neighborhood because I've never seen it before today.

I was about to walk into the building when I heard, "How you doing, Miss Lady?" I ignored the cat call and kept walking. "Oh you not gon speak to an old friend?" When I turned around to cuss my stalker out, I found that the window was rolled completely down and I was now able to see who the driver was.

"What are you doing here, boy?" I was trying to keep from smiling but I had to admit he was a sight for sore eyes.

"I came to see you." He smoothly smiled back.

"How are you, Rico?" I looked around and then walked over to his car. He opened the door and

started to get out of the car. "No, don't get out," I blurted out, looking around again.

"I heard your peoples was away at the moment, so what is the problem?" he asked, getting out of his car anyway.

"Is that right? And what else did Yvette tell you?"

He started laughing. "What makes you think Yvette told me anything? What you don't think I could have found out where you lived at on my own?"

"Hell no, so stop it!" I started laughing.

"It's really good to see you, Sabrina. You been doing a'ight?" Rico genuinely asked.

"I don't know. How did Yvette say I was doing when you saw her?" I slyly replied.

"She told me that you had been depressed since I left Virginia and for me to hurry up and come see you," he answered with a smart tone. Rico was being just as smart as I was. I could smell his cologne from where I was standing. I told myself not to get too close to him because as horny as I was, I might rape him in the parking lot.

"Oh, she did?" I asked with a smirk on my face.

"Naw, let me stop. I couldn't come to Virginia and not look you up," he answered, "and I must say you are still looking good, Sabrina."

"Thank you," I replied even though I didn't agree with him.

"Why don't you let me take you out to dinner or something?" he offered.

"I can't do that, Rico." I looked around the neighborhood again to see if anyone was watching us.

"Why not," he asked with a more serious tone.

"Because my momma will be here soon to drop my daughter off, that's why."

"How is our daughter . . . I mean your daughter doing?"

"That's not funny, Rico." I reached in my purse and took out my cell phone when I felt it vibrating. I didn't recognize the number so I pressed ignore and sent it to voicemail. Then, I looked back at Rico. "I told you she was not your child so I truly hope that's not why you came back to Virginia."

"I came back to Virginia to see you, Sabrina."

I felt my cellphone vibrate again and it was the same number calling me. "I need to answer this," I told him. "Hello," I spoke into the phone.

"Sabrina?"

"Who is this?" I asked.

"The fuck you mean who is this? How many other niggas call yo' phone?" It was Milk. I put my index finger up to my lips and shook my head signaling to Rico for him not to say anything.

"I'm not used to you calling me straight through like this." I walked away from Rico so I could talk to Milk. "Who did you get to call me on three-way?"

"We not on a three-way call and I don't have a lot of time to talk. Let me speak to Saysha," Milk quickly said.

"My momma hasn't dropped her off yet." I turned around when I saw that Rico was walking towards me out of the corner of my eye. "She should be here soon." Rico reached out to me as if he were going to take the phone away from me. I put my hand on the receiver. "Stop playing," I whispered, starting to walk backwards.

"Do what?" I heard Milk say.

"Nothing. I was talking to the next door neighbor." I lied.

"You just now getting home?" Milk asked.

"Yeah, I just got off the bus." Rico started tickling me and I couldn't help but laugh.

"Whatchu' laughing at," Milk asked. I popped Rico on his arm and gave him another wide eyed look while shaking my head at him again to stop. I cleared my throat.

"These kids out here playing." I pointed at Rico who was still laughing.

"Well look, I'mma' try to call you back in a couple of hours so I can talk to my Saysha," he said.

"Okay."

"I love you."

"You, too," I told him.

"Whatchu' mean, you too?" he asked with an attitude. Rico was standing directly in front of me and it made me hesitant to tell Milk that I loved him back, but I knew if I didn't there would be a problem.

"I love you, too," I said. Rico looked away from me in obvious disappointment.

"I was 'bout to say," he said. "I'll talk to you later."

"Okay, bye." I pressed end on my phone and put it back inside my purse.

"How Milk doing?" Rico asked.

"Like you really care. . ." I felt my phone vibrate and I thought it may have been Milk calling again, but when I looked at it I saw that it was my momma. "Don't say anything Rico and I'm not playing," I told him, before answering the phone. "Hello?"

"Hey, I'mma' keep Saysha here with me tonight." My momma took her to the doctor today for me so I didn't have to miss my class and it turned out Saysha had an ear infection.

"No, Ma, bring her home. My baby sick and I want to be the one to take care of her," I whined.

"I wasn't calling you to ask for your permission. I was just letting you know so you wouldn't be looking for me," my momma said with a little sass.

I started laughing and shook my head. "Y'all are going to stop kidnapping my child. You and Aunt Neicy are terrible!"

"Shut up before I don't bring her back until Sunday. Good-bye!" She abruptly hung up the phone.

"So I guess that means I won't get to see my baby, huh?" Rico said with a grin on his face.

"I told you that she was not your child so you need to stop saying that." Rico was starting to irritate me now.

"Honestly, how do you know that? We ain't never take a blood test," Rico responded, leaning up against his car.

"Because I just do," I rolled my eyes at him.

"Let me see this for a minute," he said, snatching my cell phone out of my hand.

"I'm sure you have your own cell phone," I said, reaching for my phone.

"Hold up a second," he said, starting to dial a number. When I heard his cell phone ringing I knew then what he was doing. "Here you go." He passed my phone back to me. "Now we can keep in touch with one another." He bit down on his bottom lip.

"And why would we want to do that?" I asked.

"What? We can't be friends?"

"I don't think friendship is all that you are looking for," I frankly said.

"Yes it is," Rico said, opening his car door. "For right now."

I stood there and watched him drive away until his car could no longer be seen from where I was standing. I dialed Yvette's number as I walked back towards the building, but as usual her voicemail picked up on the first ring.

"Juju," I called out to my cousin as I entered the apartment. When he didn't respond I called his name again. "Juju!" I could hear music coming from his bedroom so I knew he was home, plus his car was outside. I put my purse down on the kitchen table and then walked towards his bedroom. "Juju?" I knocked on the door. As loud as the music was it was no wonder he couldn't hear me. I opened the door and poked my head in.

"How can I . . . ease the pain . . . when I know you're coming back again... how can I ease the pain in my heart. . ."

Juju was lying down on the bed on his side with a box of tissues beside him. He and Mike broke up a week ago and he has not left the house, let alone his bedroom, since.

"Juju, you alright?" I walked into the room and sat down at the foot of his bed. I picked up the remote to his stereo and turned the music down. "You want to talk about it?" I sat the remote down on the bed as he sat up.

"No I don't want to talk about nothing . . . *sniff.* . . *sniff* . . . I'm just going to stay in my room, in my bed, and suffer in silence . . . *sniff* . . . *sniff.* . ." He wiped his eyes with a Kleenex.

"Juju, less than two weeks ago, you were telling me that life goes on and to roll with it. Now look at you. Sitting in hear listening to sad love songs and shit."

"I know . . . *sniff* . . . *sniff.* . ." he agreed with me. "Let me put on something else." He picked up the remote and pressed a button.

"And I am telling you . . . I'm not going . . . you're the best man I've ever known . . . and there's no way. . ."

"Juju," I looked at him.

"You don't like that song either . . . *sniff* . . .," he asked.

"No."

The next selection was Adele's *'Rolling In The Deep'*, and as soon as she got to the chorus he broke down and started crying again. I took the remote away from him and turned the music completely off. It wasn't funny because I know how Juju felt about Mike, but it was taking everything in me not to laugh at his dramatic antics.

"Juju," I looked at him. "I'mma' need you to pull it together." I sat the remote down on the dresser out of his reach. "This is so not you." I scooted over close to him so that I could give him a hug.

"I should go to his house and bust every last motha-fuck-in' window out of his car. Yeah . . . that's what I should do," he whined. "I knew something was going on with him and that jealous bitch Tyree . . . *sniff* . . . *sniff* . . . I just knew it." Juju rolled his eyes before letting out a whale of a sob. "My mind don't fool me, Sabrina. I can spot a jealous bitch a mile away. You know what I'm saying?" I thought he was about to haul off and start balling crying the way he was carrying on. "I gave Mike the best year off my life . . . *sniff* . . . *sniff.*"

"Well, do you think you can forgive him and give him another chance?" I rubbed his back while still trying not to fall out laughing at the dramatics.

"Absolutely not!" Juju quickly stopped crying and pressed his lips together. "Not today, not tomorrow, not ever!"

"I'm sorry, Juju." I rubbed his shoulder. "Its gon' be alright." When I said that he started crying again. *'Lord have mercy,'* I thought. "I'm cooking tonight and I'm going to make some of your favorites"

"Whatchu' gon' cook bitch?" Juju looked at me with puppy dog eyes as he attempted to stop crying. He wiped tears from his eyes and patted his face rapidly with a Kleenex.

"It's a surprise, but while I'm cooking I want you to get up out of this bed and go take you a shower. Cause like you once told me, 'you look wretched girlfriend,' and that is not my Juju. Don't he know that you are the fiercest bitch on earth?" I plucked my fingers and finally saw a spark in Juju's eyes. "Mike must got you fucked up, honey!"

"You're just saying that!" He waved his hand at me and wiped his eyes again with the tissue in his hand.

"I'm not just saying that. Juju you know can't nobody compare to you on your worst day." I knew how to comfort my cousin; stroke his ego. "Somebody better ask about you." I rolled my neck.

Unfortunately, even that didn't work. I had to bring his food to him after I cooked because he still would not come out of his room, but he ate that food faster than Shug Avery did when Ms. Celie cooked for her in the movie *The Color Purple*. Juju's behavior went on for another week before he and Mike were back together, and to show Juju how sorry he was for what he did Mike brought him a

 Rayven Skyy

new car. I guess gay men are just like straight men when it comes to guilt gifts. I guess it benefitted us both because Juju told me that I could drive his car so that I didn't have to take the bus anymore. Thank you, Jesus!

All Seeing Eye!

Sabrina's letters slowed down after we got into it about Nicole. I went from getting three or four a week to barely even getting one, but that only lasted for a few weeks. She just don't know she really ain't got shit to worry about when I come home as far as Nicole is concerned. I'm broker than this country and I know how Nicole roles. No money, no talk what so ever.

I did fuck Nicole a few times after me and Sabrina got back together when she told me that she was pregnant. Let me be the one to tell you fellas in case you don't know, the only thing in this world better than pussy is pregnant pussy and you know I couldn't let that pass me by. Nicole was a willing participant as long as I threw her a few extra dollars on top of the money that I was already giving her.

I never told Sabrina that I was going to Nicole's doctor appointments with her either. I told her I wasn't going to do anything as far as the baby was concerned until I had a blood test done, but I didn't want to make the same mistake I did with Deshawn even though he turned out not to be my son. I wanted to be there from day one. Besides, I missed out on a lot when Sabrina was pregnant so I guess I was trying to make up for that with Mj.

I don't know how Sabrina is going to feel about this but once I get released. I plan on eventually having my son come live with us. I'm not saying that Nicole is a bad mother, despite all of the shit Sabrina tells me she has heard about her. I saw for myself a long time ago when she first started bringing Mj up here to see me how she was with him. For some reason she always acted like she didn't want to hold him. Once I was in the visiting room and as soon as I sat down she would pass him to me.

When babies start crying mommas don't care if the daddy is the one holding him, they will eventually take the baby from him if he cries too long. Not Nicole. She sat there and acted like she ain't heard shit. Even when I went to her doctor appointments she didn't seem the least bit excited when she heard the baby's heart beat or even when she was getting the ultrasound and found out that she was having another boy. She didn't even crack a smile.

I used to ask Nicole about her other son, Bre, and when was he coming back to live with her but she would never give me a straight answer. To me, Nicole comes across like an emotionless person. Even after the shit with Gremlin she was shaken up for a minute, but that quickly went away.

All know is I'm ready to get the fuck from out of here and go home, but right now it looks like home will be the last place I want to live in. Especially not in Virginia Beach at Carriage House!

Sabrina told me a few months ago that she put in an application and got on the waiting list, and recently she found out that she was approved for a two bedroom apartment that she would not have to pay any rent for. Carriage House was close to my old stomping ground, Broad Meadows. It was a neighborhood me, my nigga Kirk, and my brother Rell moved to after Kirk's momma died. I've fucked quite a few broads that lived out at Carriage House, so I know the "All Seeing Eye" known as Sabrina will be watching my ass like a hawk.

I only have a few months to go and I'm going to have to figure out some kind of way to make me some money. I can't just jump right back out there in the streets because the Feds may still be watching, and I'm not going to give them a reason to fuck with me.

Babies in Tow!

Thelma and Louise, a.k.a. my momma and Aunt Neicy, have kidnapped Saysha once again and took her with them to Emporia for Aunt Neicy's family reunion. I didn't put up a fuss this time because with Saysha being gone it gave me a chance to start packing. Juju is in Maryland for a hair show and won't be back until next Friday. This was the first time since I have been living with him that I actually had the apartment to myself, and I was enjoying the peace and quiet until it was interrupted by my ringing cell phone. "Thank you, Jesus," I said aloud to myself, before answering the phone. It was Yvette.

It has been at least two months since I last heard from her and I was really starting to become worried. She said her car broke down, and she was stranded out in Ocean View, and needed a ride. It boggles me that she even set foot out in Ocean View after she was brutally beaten in that drug infested neighborhood.

Yvette stayed clean for six months once she was released from the hospital. I don't know what triggered her relapse, but ever since then her drug use has been out of control. Nonetheless, when I was going through my ordeal last year Yvette was right there for me so I have to be there for her. It was no problem for me to hop in my car and go to her rescue like I have done so many times before.

I turned into the strip mall that Yvette told me to pick her up from. I didn't see her standing around anywhere so I parked the car and dialed her cell phone number, but her voicemail picked up on the first ring. "Really, 'Vette," I asked aloud. I hung up and then tried calling her for a second time, but her voicemail greeted me again. "Damn that girl!" I shook my head to myself. Luckily I had the window rolled down and was able to hear her calling my name before I pulled out of the shopping center. "I tried calling your phone," I told her when she got inside the car.

"I let a friend use my car and forgot to get my charger," she said, getting inside and closing the door. Yvette smelled just as bad as that girl Tanisha from my Workforce class, and with all the plaque built up in between her teeth I knew that bathing wasn't the only thing she was neglecting to do. Lord, what is happening to my best friend?

"You let a friend use what?" I questioned.

"Use my car," she responded nonchalantly.

"Yvette, I thought you said your car was broke down? And put your seat belt on," I told her. She put the seatbelt on but still hadn't answered my question. "Ain't that what you told me on the phone, that your car was broke down?"

"Sabrina, just drive." She motioned with her hand trying to evade the question.

"Drive where?" I asked, with my foot still on the brake.

"I'm going to Park Place," she quickly responded. Park Place was another neighborhood in Norfolk not too far from Ocean View that was also a high crime area.

"You're going out Park Place for what?" I asked with an agitated tone, putting the car in park.

"I'm going over my cousin's house."

I knew she was lying. Yvette didn't have any relatives that lived out in Park Place that I knew of. "What cousin?" I raised my voice.

"My cousin Shana!" she yelled back.

"Oh, now you have a cousin name Shana that lives out Park Place ten minutes from where we grew up together? I have never heard you mention her before nor have I met her." I folded my arms across my chest. I felt like I was talking to a teenager talking to Yvette.

"Sabrina, you don't know everybody in my damn family!"

"The only place that I am taking you is home! I don't care what you say." I put the car back in drive and pulled off.

"You can't take me home because I don't live there anymore," Yvette stammered.

"What?" I sharply looked over at her and then turned my focus back to the road.

"I said I don't live there anymore. Just take me where I asked you to please if that's alright with you."

"Yvette, did you get put out your condo?" I didn't bother to look in her direction again because her silence spoke volumes. "Where have you been staying?"

"Sabrina, why are you always asking me so many questions," Yvette whined.

"Because I care about, Yvette, that's why."

Yvette never responded and we rode in silence back to Juju's apartment. She didn't question me as to where I was taking her, and within ten minutes her head was leaned up against the window as she slept. I took a good look at her for the first time in months and I could see that the streets were starting to take a toll on her. I know that I am a house guest and I shouldn't be inviting anyone else to Juju's place to stay, but the last place I was going to take Yvette was out to Park Place and her momma's house was not an option either. Yvette burned that bridge when she stole money and two credit cards from her.

When we finally made it to the apartment, I went in my room to get some clothes for Yvette to put on and told her to go take a shower while I fixed her something to eat. I also gave her a tooth brush so that she could brush her teeth. I kept my purse close to me, and when I moved my purse did, too. After she came out of the bathroom I started to tell her to give me the clothes she had on so I could throw them in the trash, but instead I told her to put them on top of the washing machine in the hallway and I would wash them for her later.

"By the way, why the hell did you tell Rico where I lived?" I asked Yvette, collecting our plates after we finished eating and putting them in the sink. You would have thought this was Yvette's last supper by the way she ate her food so fast. I could tell that she had not eaten in days.

"I didn't. . ." I turned around and gave Yvette a *'bitch, please'* look before she could get the lie she was about to tell me out of her mouth.

"Yes you did, Yvette," I challenged, cutting her off. "You know Virginia Beach ain't that big. Suppose somebody had seen me with him and it got back to Milk?" Now that he has access to a cell phone it's no telling who Milk is talking to.

"Sorry," she said nonchalantly.

"*Sorry,*" I jabbed, mocking her. "He gave you some money didn't he?" Yvette didn't answer and her silence was a dead giveaway that I was right once again. "Girl, I don't believe you!" I shook my head and Yvette started to cry, but I was hip to the waterworks game at this point so her tears did not faze me one bit. "Yvette, you got to get it together, baby."

"I know," she whispered. I passed her a paper towel to wipe her face with. "I want to Sabrina, I really do," she said, blowing her nose into the paper towel.

I grabbed my purse off of the counter, went into the living room, and sat down on the sofa. A few minutes later Yvette came and joined me, but not long after that she was asleep again. I got a blanket out the hall closet, laid it across her, and followed suit shortly after. I woke up in the middle of the night to check to see if she was still there because I was for certain she would end up leaving before morning now that she had something to eat and a few hours of sleep, but she made a liar out of me when I saw that she was still on the couch.

I was awakened by my cell phone early the next morning. I assumed it was Milk calling me since it was Saturday and the phones were back on, but it wasn't him calling me. It was Juju. He decided to stay in Maryland for another week and it would be after the fifth before he came home, so he told me to take the money out of his top drawer to pay the rent and the light bill with. I was still half asleep as I listened to Juju, but as soon as I heard him say the word money I quickly flung the covers off me and raced to his room.

I told Juju to hold on and laid my cell phone down on top of his dresser. I turned the light on and opened his top drawer. I frantically went through the drawer and some of Juju's male thongs fell on the floor. I pulled the drawer out, turned it over, and dumped everything out on the bed. '*Oh my God!*'

I ran into the living room, but unlike the last time I checked on her Yvette was gone and so was the rent and light bill money. When I got back on the phone with Juju I lied and told him that I had the money and would make sure everything was taken care of. As the words came out of my mouth

I started to think about who I could get the money from. I went back into my room, sat down on the side of the bed, and took a long, deep breath. I had no idea Juju even kept money in the house like that or I would have locked his room door.

I laid on my back for a minute staring up at the ceiling when I thought about my own money. I sat up and looked on the side of the bed and my purse was gone. I felt like the wind had been knocked out of me. Not only did I have to get twelve hundred dollars to pay the rent, plus money for the light bill but now I had to replace the twenty dollars I did have in my purse that I was going to use to by some Pull Ups for Saysha. I have borrowed enough money from momma and daddy and I didn't want to get any more money from either one of them. I would cut my right arm off before I asked my sister for a nickel!

I got up and went into the bathroom to wash my face and brush my teeth, and when I turned the light on I was surprised to see that my purse was on the side of the toilet stool sitting on the floor. I picked it up even though I already knew the money was gone. As I started going through it to see what else was missing, it came to me who I could get some money from and I knew what I was going to have to do to get it.

Like I've heard my momma say many times before, "Never say what you won't do when you have babies in tow."

Lay it to Rest!

I was confident that Sabrina would eventually contact me, but I didn't expect it to be so soon. I told her that I was staying at The Westin in the Towne Center area of Virginia Beach and that she could come there to get the money she needed, but she didn't want to risk running into anybody she knew. I started to tell her "Fuck Milk," but I didn't want to piss her off and blow my chance at seeing her again.

I told Sabrina if she was that worried about being seen that she could meet me up at the park I used to meet Gremlin at. She didn't tell me what she needed the money for, but she really didn't have to. If there was one person in this world that could get anything from me it was Sabrina. I knew it would work in my favor in the long run, which was approximately a week after I had given her the money.

Since the hotel that I was staying in was in Sabrina's neck of the woods, I told her I would get another one across the water in Hampton and stay there until I went back to Miami. She made it clear to me that she was not going to leave Milk and when he came home we would have to cut all contact off with each other. I told her that I was only going to be in town for a couple more weeks

 Rayven Skyy

and she didn't have to worry about me causing any trouble for her. From there we were able to pick right up where we left off the last time we saw each other, and to my delight Sabrina's pussy still curved to fit my dick like a hand in a glove and her clit still got as hard as a jellybean. Still no luck as far as head was concerned, but Sabrina told me the first time I ever slept with her that she wasn't into that which was cool with me since at the time I was only using her to get closer to Milk. If we would've ended up being together later on in life that no head shit would have become an issue for me.

Tonight I took Sabrina out to dinner. As I sat there waiting for her to come out of the bathroom, I thought about the pictures she showed me of her daughter. I can put that theory to rest that she could possibly be my baby because there was no denying that she was that nigga's child. Saysha looked like a light-skinned Milk with ponytails, but I have to admit it made me feel some kind of way because Sabrina had not taken a blood test and I held on to the hope that she could possibly be mine.

Some things changed about Sabrina that I took notice of. She seemed more humbled and I'm sure the drastic change in her lifestyle played a part in her transformation, but the one thing that had not changed was how beautiful she was, even with her hair slicked back in a ponytail. I was used to seeing her in expensive clothes and wearing more jewelry than Mr. T, but tonight she wasn't wearing anything.

I saw her come out of the bathroom and walk towards the booth we had in the back of the restaurant, and after I paid the bill we left. I knew that she wouldn't be open for doing anything else tonight because it was getting late so I headed back to the hotel.

"Where did you get the name Saysha from?" I asked Sabrina. When I looked over at her in the passenger's seat the street lights cast a glow that radiated her skin.

"From this girl I used to go to school with. The first time I heard that name I said if I ever had a little girl I would name her that." She smiled.

"How you spell it? Y'all women can get crazy when it comes to that. Some of these kids won't be able to graduate from kindergarten 'cause they can't pronounce their names or spell it either." We both started laughing.

"I see you're still a comedian. When are you going on tour with Kevin Hart?"

"I'm just waiting on the phone call." I winked at her.

"S-a-y-s-h-a is how I spelled it and I only threw the y in there so people would not mispronounce it and call her Sasha. That's simple enough, right?" Sabrina happily asked.

"If you say so," I shook my head just to annoy her.

"Shut up, Rico!" She laughed and punched me on my arm.

"Oh, ain't nothing changed," I said, teasing her. "I will still call the police on you if you put your hands on me."

"Well what if I put my hands on this," she asked, running her hand along my thigh. "Or what if I put my hands on this?"

"I could give you a get out of jail free card when you put your hands on Byrd, Jr." I flashed Sabrina a sly grin.

"Really. Can you buy the boardwalk for me then, too?" Sabrina said with a very flirtatious tone.

"I'll buy you California if that's what you told me you wanted." I know Sabrina could tell by the change in my facial expression that I meant what I just said. "I'm serious." I nodded my head forward. "Sabrina, you can have anything I got."

"Rico . . ." I already knew what she was going to say by the way she said my name.

"Sabrina . . ." I said in my white girl voice, and she started to laugh again.

"Boy, something is wrong with you."

I took Sabrina's hand, raised it up to my lips, and kissed the back of it. "I know what time it is 'cause you already put it out there in the universe that you gon' be with the nigga, and besides," I kissed her hand again, "Plus, I'm tired of being a home wrecker. Sabrina snatched her hand away and punched me on my arm again.

"Boy, fuck you!" she said, continuing to laugh.

"Come on then . . ." I sat all the way up in my seat and then pressed my foot on the gas pedal. I knew what I was looking for I just had to find it. I wasn't as familiar with Hampton as I was Virginia Beach so it took me a little longer to find what I was looking for. I turned off the headlights and made a right.

"Rico, why are you turning into this school parking lot?" Sabrina looked around and then back at me.

"You said you wanted to fuck me," I said, driving towards the back of the school building. "So I'mma' let you fuck me."

"I know you seriously do not think that I am going to have sex with you in your car?"

"Of course not, why would you say that?"

"And we aren't doing it outside in the back of a school building either," she sharply stated, looking at me with her head tilted to the side.

"I know that. If we get caught we could fuck around and catch an indecent exposure charge."

"So why are we here then?"

"Since you said you wanted to fuck me, I'm going to let you fuck me on that." I pointed.

"On what? The school bus?" Now she was pointing, too.

"This is my last night in Virginia and no telling if I'm gon' ever see you again. Look at it as a parting gift."

"You're serious aren't you?" Sabrina looked at me like I was crazy.

"Or consider it a see you later gift then." I had her laughing again.

"Okay. A see you later gift." She stopped laughing and kissed me on the lips.

I parked behind a dumpster so my car could not be seen and turned off the ignition. "Come on," I told her. Sabrina and I got out of the car at the same time and I waited for her to walk over to the other side so that I could hold her hand.

"How are we going to get on the bus anyway?" she asked. She then started looking back as we walked toward the buses.

"You must not be a spontaneous person."

"I'm spontaneous . . . It's just that I have been to jail before and I would prefer not going back."

"Girl, ain't nobody going to jail. Come on here." I tugged on her hand to pull her along.

"You still didn't tell me how we were supposed to get on the bus. Don't they have locks on them? I know you're not going to break the windows are you?"

"Nope. We not gon' to have to break shit, because the doors are already open." I let go of Sabrina's hand and pried the doors all the way open. "After you, Ms. Spontaneous." Sabrina looked back one more time before she stepped up on the bus and when she did I smacked her on the ass.

"Owww . . ." she whined.

"Shut up!" I hit her again. "You like it," I playfully stated, lowering my tone. I grabbed

Sabrina by her waist so she would stop walking and pulled her toward me. "Don't you?" I brushed my dick up against her.

"Like what?"

"You like it when I get a little rough."

"When have you ever been rough with me, Rico?" Sabrina turned around and looked at me.

"Now!" Before she could react I turned Sabrina back around and I had her bent over with her hands lying flat on the seat. She was wearing a skirt and that made it easier for me to get to what I wanted. "That's because I have always made love to you, but not tonight. Since you want to fuck that's what we gon do."

"Is that right?" she seductively asked.

"Damn right." I pulled her panties down below her thighs. Then I reached inside my pocket, got the last condom out of the three pack box, tore it open, and put it on. Sabrina has been very adamant about us using condoms this time and I know she is not going to let it slide just because I was leaving town. "Why you so quiet?" I asked, leaning down and whispering in her ear.

"What do you want me to say?"

"It ain't what I want you to say, it's what I want to hear." Without warning I thrust my dick so far inside of her that she almost fell over in the seat.

"Ahhhh . . ." she loudly moaned.

"That's the sound I want to hear!"

I continued to pound myself in and out of Sabrina's walls and her moans became louder and

 Rayven Skyy

her breathing became heavier. Milk might as well put some flowers on her pussy and lay it to rest when he comes home because I just killed it!

Apt B!

2 months later . . .

I was able to keep in touch with Maine once my cell mate, Pound, got his hands on a cell phone. I asked him to come and pick me up once I was released from prison. He took me to the mall and bought me a few outfits, a couple pair of shoes. I was expecting him to throw a couple of dollars my way since I was just coming home, but Maine just got out of jail not too long ago himself on an assault charge.

I did ask him to stop by Nicole's crib on my way to Carriage House so that I could see Mj. I told Nicole I would be back to get him the next day after I came back from seeing my probation officer. Maine asked me if I wanted to go to the strip club tonight, but I told him I was chilling and would get with him sometime tomorrow, plus I wasn't going nowhere without no money in my pocket.

"Who is it?"

"It's me," I answered.

"Who?"

"Milk!"

I heard the top lock turn, then the bottom, and the door slightly opened, but the chain on the door kept it from opening all the way.

"Sabrina here," I asked.

"Hold on for a second," she said, shutting the door in my face. *'What the fuck?'* When I realized that she closed the door so that she could take the chain off I quickly calmed down. Once the door opened again a girl wearing a pair of cut off shorts and a halter top with no shoes on was standing in the doorway.

"Sabrina here," I asked again.

"Sabrina doesn't live here." She smiled.

"Whatchu' mean she don't live here? This is apartment B right?" I looked above the door frame to make sure I was at the right apartment.

"Yeah, this is apartment B," she answered, still smiling. "Sabrina lives in the next building in apartment B."

"Oh shit," I started laughing. "My bad."

"It's alright. You need me to walk you over there?" She looked me up and down with *'I want to fuck you'* eyes.

"Naw, I think I'm good." I turned around to walk out of the building.

"Well, my name is Tonikia." I turned around and discovered that she had pulled her halter top down. Two of the most succulent set of titties I have seen in a long time were now looking back at me. After being locked up for over a year to see any part of a broad naked will immediately send blood rushing to your dick, and I was no exception. Let me get the fuck out this hallway before I get in some trouble already. "If you ever need anything don't hesitate to knock on my door and ask," she said, pulling her top back up when the door across the hall from her apartment opened.

"A'ight!" I laughed again and walked out of the building. As soon as I did I heard a familiar voice calling for me.

"Daddy, Daddy!" It was Saysha and she was running towards me. Sabrina was standing on the porch to the right of the building I just came out of.

"There go daddy baby," I said, picking her up. "I love you," I told her, as I kissed her on the lips.

"I love you too, Daddy. You wanna go to the park wit' me, Daddy?" she asked, pointing to the play area of the park across the street.

"Daddy will take you over there later on, okay?" I put her down, took her by the hand, and walked towards Sabrina. I don't know why but for some reason I was starting to feel nervous. I felt like I had something jumping around in my stomach. *'This is Sabrina. What the fuck am I nervous about?'*

"Hey you," Sabrina said. We embraced each other and then I leaned down and kissed her on the lips. The butterfly feeling intensified as I followed Sabrina into her building while still holding Saysha's hand.

"Wanna' see my room, Daddy?" Saysha excitedly said.

"I sure do wanna see my baby room. Show it to me," I responded like a proud father.

"Okay," she said with excitement. "Dis' way."

My tour guide started pulling me by my hand and I followed her into the apartment and then her room. Not only was my stomach really starting to feel fucked up, but looking around Sabrina's apartment made my heart race and I felt awkward. Even though I had been in these apartments out in Carriage House before I forgot how small they were. Our bedroom in our old house was bigger than this whole apartment!

There wasn't much furniture in what was considered to be the living room, and I'm sure it had been given to Sabrina by somebody because I knew she has not had the money to buy furniture. Saysha's room, which I could see from the living room, was the best room in the apartment just like in our last house. There were two twin beds in her room, a dresser, a big Dora toy box, and a Dora chair and table set. Pretty much everything in the room was accented with the pie face little girl.

"Come on, Daddy, dis' way," she said, as if we had far to walk. "Sit down!" She pulled out one of the little chairs to her table set.

"This chair too small for Daddy, I might break it." I started laughing. I turned around to see where Sabrina was and found that she was sitting on the couch in the living room. I was wondering if she could sense how uncomfortable I was.

Two Dora videos later, my movie date had fallen asleep in my lap. I laid her down on the bed that we were sitting on and closed the door behind me. I poked my head in Sabrina's bedroom to see what it looked like. There was a Queen sized bed without a headboard that took up most of the room, a dresser, and a stand with an old model TV sitting on it. *'Damn! Look how my baby has been living.'*

I walked to the kitchen, which only took a few steps for me to get there from Sabrina's bedroom, when I heard water running. Sabrina was standing at the sink washing dishes. I stood in the door way because the kitchen was not big enough to me for both of us to be in. I noticed that there was a Virginia Power electric bill on the refrigerator being held in place with magnets. She must have seen me standing there out of the corner of her eye because she turned and looked at me.

"What's wrong?" she asked, turning off the water.

"Nothing," I shook my head trying to be calm.

"Where is Saysha?"

"She fell asleep."

"You hungry? You want something to drink?" she asked.

"Naw, I'm good," I said, lying my ass off. The food I had earlier was long gone and I was hungry as a mothafucka', but I still couldn't shake the uncomfortable feeling. "I'm not used to this." I said

to myself as I looked around the tiny apartment. "I'm not used to this shit at all."

Step Mother!

I could tell by the look on his face when he walked inside my apartment that Milk wasn't too pleased with our current living situation. His eyes darted from corner to corner as he looked around at everything. I'm just hoping and praying that he does not jump right back out into the streets.

I must admit it hasn't been an easy adjustment and Carriage House may be a downgrade from where we used to live, but if it means I would not have to look over my shoulder for the rest of my life or think that everybody who walks past me is an undercover police officer I will stay right where I am. If anybody had warned me ahead of time about everything that was going to happen, I would have gladly traded it all not to have to go through what both Milk and I did. In some ways I know that it had an effect on Saysha, too.

The following day after Milk came home Maine took him to go see his probation officer and to pick up Mj, which was actually four days ago. We talked about this a few months before he came home and I told Milk that I didn't have a problem with his son coming to my house. I can't say that I was thrilled with the idea of being somebody's step mother when Milk got his blood test results back, but I would much rather he go pick him up than be

sitting up under Nicole's ass. I don't know what kind of mother she calls herself.

Milk does not have a cell phone but he told me that he was going to give Nicole the house number and that bitch hasn't called to check on her baby yet. I guess everything Juju told me he heard about Nicole's parenting skills must've been true. To tell you the truth, Mj is actually a good baby. The only time he gets fussy is when he does not have that pacifier in his mouth, and for him to be almost fourteen months you would think Nicole would've weaned him off of it by now. You can tell he sits in either a carrier or swing often by the bald spot in the back of his head. Poor thing! I should call child protective services and report her ass.

Passing the Torch!

I made sure I sent plenty of clothes, pampers, and milk for Mj when Milk came to pick him up. I went shopping . . . well shit, ain't no need for me to lie. You know how I get down. I had to upgrade Mj's wardrobe before I sent him over to that bitch's house. I thought I would remind Sabrina what name brand clothes looked like just in case she had forgotten. Needless to say, Milk doesn't call me and I don't know what the hell he gave me Sabrina's cell phone number for because I had no intentions of calling him. For what? I'm passing the torch and it's his turn to change shitty pampers. Now I know what Martin Luther King, Jr. meant when he said, "free at last," because thank God almighty Nicole is free at last! Now... back to me!

First on the agenda is to find my next sponsor. Now that Milk is broke, which does not look good on him I might add, I am certain he has been replaced out in the streets. Like a blood hound chasing a runaway slave I know how to sniff them out, but I may not have to. Angelle's boyfriend, Onion, came up to the shop the other day to bring her something to eat and I could smell the money on him.

Angelle don't know what to do with him because she still walking around dressed like she

 Rayven Skyy

gets her clothes from Thrift Stores R'Us, so that tells me she ain't hitting them pockets right. Why not just take him off her hands? She ain't about this life.

Miss New Booty!

"Yeah, man. I'm so mad at the streets right now I could kill something," Maine said, as we cruised down High Street.

"Shit that bad out here?" I asked, looking out the window.

"Man, what?" Maine glanced at me. "When the Feds snatched you up niggas was hurting for a minute and dope was scarce as a mothafucka'. I heard about the nigga we going to meet up with when I was in jail, and from what I hear he has some reasonable prices."

"Oh yeah?"

I was still looking out of the window. We were on our way to Forbidden City, a strip club in the downtown section of Portsmouth, a city twenty minutes away from Virginia Beach. This was the first time that I really hung out since I have been home, and even though Sabrina said that she didn't mind watching Mj I still felt funny leaving him there with her. I don't want to put much on her because Saysha is a handful by herself, and that's why I'm not going to stay out too late.

"Just be careful who you fuck with man with these snitchin' ass mothafuckas' 'round here," I added. I wished it was me who was going to meet up with somebody to get some work, but right now

I can't take any chances. "Who is this nigga anyway?" I looked at Maine.

"Some nigga Onion fuck with. Matter of fact, he bought Forbidden City a few months ago," he answered.

"Onion? You talking 'bout the nigga who fucked up Yvette?"

"Yeah, man. Lee told me that this nigga and Onion took over the streets the OG way by bodying niggas left and right."

"I know you got yo' burner on you right?" I had not seen Onion since I whipped his ass for what he did to Yvette. I may be broke but I will still kill a mothafucka' if I have to.

"Man, I already hollered at Onion 'bout that shit 'cause I knew he would be in this mothafucka' tonight and shit is cool. Right now niggas just trying to eat!" Maine turned into the shopping center and drove towards the strip club.

"What the fuck? That's Forbidden City?" I pointed at the club.

"Yeah, man. The nigga remodeled that mothafucka' inside and out and it be packed in here, too. Security is tight." Maine parked the car and we got out.

"I don't give a fuck how tight it is! If the nigga come at me sideways I'mma go to his ass again. Give me yo' gun man." I held out my hand as we walked towards the club entrance.

"Man, I left that shit in the car. They got metal detectors in this mothafucka' and ain't nobody getting no hammers in here. And besides, yo' name still carry a lot of weight in the streets so niggas know what time it is. Come on man so you can get yo' dick sucked after I finish handling my business." I started laughing.

"Shit, I know that's right!" I slapped hands with Maine. Sabrina did shockingly give me some head the first night I came home, but I know it will be Christmas before she gives me some again.

Maine said the security was tight in this mothafucka' and he ain't never lied. There was a metal detector at the club entrance that you had to walk through plus they still patted you down. Then there was another door that you had to go through that lead inside the club. Whoever the nigga is that bought this mothafucka' put in a lot of work.

I used to come to Forbidden City every now and then before I got locked up, but not too often because it was a hole in the wall and there wasn't a good selection of women to choose from. Now there was a VIP section, an area where they do lap dances, and a bigger stage for the dancers to perform. There were even mirrors on all the walls which made the club look even bigger.

I saw a few niggas that I knew once we were inside. They showed mad love to me and the drinks were flowing. A few of them gave me a couple of dollars to put in my pocket. I didn't want to count it right there in their faces like I needed the money, but I already knew what I was going to do with it anyway. Give it to Sabrina.

The lights over the stage were slightly dimmed. A girl walked up on stage and was now dancing to Bubba Sparks '*Miss New Booty*'. She definitely had my attention. I moved close enough so that I could see but not close enough for her to start dancing in front of me expecting me to put some money in her G-string. I used to be the tip-drill king, but shorty won't getting not one of these slugs in my pocket.

She was wearing a mask that covered her eyes so I could not see her face, but when she took the bikini top off I knew exactly who she was. I recognized those titties anywhere, especially with her name tatted across them. It was Tonikia, the girl that lived in the building next to us, and she was looking directly at me. She made her way to the front of the stage and played patty cake with her two ass cheeks as she moved to the rhythm of the music.

"Come on man, we going in VIP," Maine happily said, motioning with his head.

"Hold up nigga," I said, never taking my focus off of Tonikia who was now laying on her back with her legs wide open. She had on a thong so I couldn't actually see her pussy. Here in Virginia, that was as naked as strippers could get.

"A'ight man," Maine started laughing. "I'mma' go holla at this nigga. VIP is in over there." He pointed.

"Naw, man," I turned around to Maine before taking one last look at Tonikia. "Here I come." I sipped the last of my drink, put the glass down on the table next to me, and followed him to the back of the club. "What's up," I said, slapping hands with this nigga named Poochie that I grew up with in Tidewater Park. I passed him on my way to the VIP section and he noticed me.

We had to walk up a few stairs to get to VIP, which was not as well lit as the rest of the club, and for a second I was hesitant about going in there. I like to be able to see niggas' faces, especially knowing Onion was somewhere in this mothafucka'. Maine talks all the shit he wants but most niggas don't take too kindly to you beating their ass. Even though Maine didn't lay a hand on him, because he was with me and held a gun on the rest of the niggas who were out there that night the streets have similar laws as the state laws. Maine was guilty by association. No more drinks for me tonight. I needed to be aware of my surroundings with a clear head.

"Can I get you anything?"

"Naw, baby, I'm good," I told the topless waitress who had just walked up to me and Maine.

"The gentleman over there told me to make sure I took care of you two." She smiled at me. "I'm sure there is something I can get for you," she said, licking her lips.

"Who told you to do that?" I questioned, looking around. When I saw Onion at a table holding a drink up in the air as if he was making a toast, I answered my own question.

Sitting next to him was a nigga with a black fitted cap on but I couldn't' see his face because the brim on his hat was low. Now I really didn't want shit. Not a drink or her pussy either. I told her that I was good, but Maine told her to bring him a Ciroc on the rocks. I looked around to see if there were any other niggas up here that I may have beef with, and one thing that I noticed was there were quite a few unfamiliar faces in the crowd.

When I looked over in Onion's direction again he had his hand in the air this time motioning for me and Maine to come over to where he was sitting. I didn't' move. Not that I was scared of him or worried about him doing something to me. Fuck that nigga! Milk don't come to no mothafuckin' body. Maine walked over to where they were sitting.

When he reached the table Onion stood up and they slapped hands with each other. Onion leaned over and said something in Maine's ear, and then he turned around and said something to the nigga that was sitting beside him who stood up and slapped hands with Maine, too. I still couldn't see the nigga's face because of the hat. Maine pointed at me and they were all looking in my direction.

"You sure I can't get you anything?" The topless waitress had returned and I told her once again that I was good. When I looked back over to see where Maine was the nigga in the black fitted was walking towards me by himself, and the closer he got to me I recognized who it was. It was Byrd.

"Welcome home Milk," he said, reaching his hand out to me. "You ain't gon' leave me hanging is you?"

"Nigga fuck you!" I pointed in his face and made sure I said it loud enough over the music so he could hear me.

"The last person who said those words to me got bent over on a school bus." He smiled.

"Yeah, and what was his name?" I stared at Byrd and he started laughing.

"How the wife and kid doing?"

"Look mothafucka', obviously you were expecting me and I see you got yo' people placed strategically in here," I said as I looked around club, "so whatever yo' intentions are, get on with the shit, nigga."

"Damn, man," he said, putting his hand on his chin. "You sure know how to hold a grudge. I was hoping we could call it a truce." He put his hands up. "Gremlin not only set you up, the nigga set me up, too. We were both victims of circumstances beyond our control and being that you are just coming home I'm going to extend you an olive branch."

"Nigga, you ain't got to do a got damn thing for me!" I took a step closer to him. Byrd tipped his hat to somebody who was behind me, but I never turned around to see who it was. I wasn't going to take my eyes off of him for a second and I wasn't going out like no punk either.

"Careful now. A lot of things have changed since you have been incarcerated. There's a new sheriff in town."

A Lying Mothafucka'!

I was walking out of the kitchen carrying a bowl of ice cream when I heard the locks to the front door turn and Milk walked inside the apartment. I really wasn't expecting him to come home so early.

"Hey," I said, walking towards the bedrooms. I cracked the door open to Saysha's room to make sure the kids were still asleep, and they were. I closed her door, went into my bedroom, sat down at the foot of the bed, and started eating my ice cream. Milk walked into the room and turned the TV off.

"What are you doing?" I abruptly looked up at him. "Why did you turn off the TV?"

"Get naked," was all he said, ignoring my question about the TV.

"Do what?" I asked.

"You heard me, pull those clothes off." Milk was already stripped down to his boxer shorts.

"Wow . . . get naked? How romantic," I said, getting up to turn the TV back on.

"Whatchu' doing?"

"Basketball Wives is getting ready to come on," I said with an attitude, turning the TV back on and then sitting back down on the bed. Ever since Milk got somebody to hook the cable up I have been

trying to catch up on all of my mindless television shows.

"Fuck them bitches. Ain't none of them basketball wives for real," Milk responded, abruptly turning off the TV again. "A nigga been locked up for a year. I should be tired right now from all the fucking we should be doing!"

I can't believe he just said that. That's all we have been doing for the last two weeks since he came home was fucking. I can't even go use the bathroom without him coming in there to get a "shot" as he called it. I swear my pussy can't take no more.

"Have you been drinking?" I looked at Milk.

"Yeah, I been drinking!" He took the bowl of ice cream out of my hands. "Why you still got your clothes on is what I want to know?" Milk walked over to me and pulled the tank top that I was wearing up over my head. He started tugging on the sweat pants, and then he suddenly stopped and looked at me. "Why do you get into bed with all this shit on anyway? Not one time since I been home have you even attempted to put on something sexy for me. Getting in the bed with these fucking corduroys on. Who do you think wants to lay up next to that shit? And you talk about somebody not being romantic . . ." Milk let out a loud, ignorant laugh.

"These are not corduroys, Milk, they're sweatpants and I would have taken them off before I got in the bed. What is your problem tonight? You say you been drinking. Are you high, too?" I put my hands on my hip.

"You know what," Milk rubbed the tip of his nose with his index finger, "you don't hear so good." He was now pointing to his left ear. "So let me get a little closer so you can hear me," Milk leaned down to my ear, "if I have to tell you a third time to get naked, I'mma' act up in this mothafucka'!"

I leaned back and looked at him with my hands still on my hips. Clearly he was drunk, high, or both and I really wasn't in the mood to argue with Milk tonight. I already had my hands on my hips, so I went ahead and pulled off my sweatpants and thong at the same time, and stepped out of them. Then I moved them closer to the dresser with my foot. I turned around and crawled up to the top of the bed and laid down on my back. Milk took off his boxers and climbed into bed behind me.

"Why didn't you turn the light off before you got in the bed, Milk?" I questioned, sitting up on my elbow.

"Leave that motherfucka' on. I haven't had a chance to look at my pussy up close since I been home. Lay back," he said slyly, nudging my shoulder.

I took a deep breath and then laid back down. This nigga was starting to get on my got damn nerves. Milk put his hands on my legs and separated them. I thought that he was about to go down on me, but then I noticed that he was

actually looking at my pussy as if he was doing an examination. I sat up on my elbows again. '*What the hell is wrong with him?*'

"Milk?" He laid on top of me forcing my elbows back down.

"Milk what," he asked. I felt his hands between my legs which were now spread apart again. "Milk what," he asked for a second time. I gasped as he put one finger and then the others inside me until he couldn't fit anymore in. "What's wrong? "He dug deeper.

"That shit hurts," I sharply said, trying to wiggle his fingers out of me. Milk willingly took them out without a struggle and then grabbed me by the ankles and put them up on his shoulders.

"I bet yo' pussy do hurt," he said with a cocky attitude. I tried to take my legs down, but Milk put them back on his shoulders. "Put 'em down again!" '*Oh my gosh*', I thought to myself. I could feel Milk fumbling between my legs as he tried to make entry. "Why yo' mothafuckin' pussy so dry?" He was now trying to force his way inside of me. "Huh? Why yo' pussy won't get wet? You must not be interested."

"Milk what the hell is wrong with you!" I yelled. This was getting ridiculous now.

"Shut up before you wake them up." I looked up at Milk and he had the most evil look on his face. Something ain't right. Now finally inside of me with an aggressive grip on my legs, Milk's dick was rock hard and he wasted no time trying to dig my guts out. It was almost as if he was raping me. "You been giving my pussy away, Sabrina?" Milk was looking me sternly in the eyes. "You been giving my pussy away?" He went back to ramming his dick inside of me.

"No," I said, starting to shake my head. "Milk no!" I cried the second time.

"Don't lie. Tell me the truth. You been giving my pussy away again, haven't you?" Milk climbed off of me and sat on the side of the bed with his back to me. "And yo' pussy still dry!"

"Milk, what is wrong with you tonight?" I sat up in the bed.

"Not a got damn thing!" He turned around. The angry look he was once giving me was gone. He started putting his boxer shorts back on, along with his jeans, followed by the white t-shirt he was wearing.

"Where are you going?" I sat up on my knees.

"Don't worry 'bout where the fuck I'm going." He opened the bedroom door. "Just let me tell yo' ass something . . ." He turned around. "I just got out of prison. Don't do nothing that is going to cause me to go back." He turned the light off, walked out of the room, and closed the door behind him, and that was that.

I laid back down on my back and stared up at the ceiling, which I really couldn't see. I know Milk has to be talking about Rico, but why is he talking about Rico is the question? The last time I saw him, which was a month before Milk came home, he

told me that he was going back to Texas to check on his grandmother and then back to Miami. So why is Milk bringing him up now after all this time? Unless . . . Rico must still be in Virginia and Milk had to have seen him somewhere.

'A lying mothafucka'!'

Unfinished Business!

"Hey baby, what's up?"

"Don't 'hey baby' me, Rico!" Sabrina yelled into the phone. "What the fuck do you call yourself doing?"

"What do you mean what I call myself doing? And hello to you, too."

"Look, Rico, I know that you are still in Virginia so don't play with me," she continued to yell.

"Why you say that, baby?"

"Because you are and stop calling me baby. Don't you dare try and start up some bullshit now that Milk is home and I mean it!" Sabrina sounded as if she was scolding a child.

"Fuck that nigga!" I responded with a yell of my own.

"Oh my God, I can't believe you," she said lowering her voice. "I should have known better than to start messing around with you again. You've been in Virginia all along haven't you?"

"Not exactly. I did leave town but I decided to come back. I had some unfinished business here."

"And what's that?"

"You," I told her.

"What about me?"

"Let's talk about this face to face, the telephone is so impersonal," I responded, trying to be funny.

"Why, so you can go back and tell Milk? I don't think so. Just do us all a favor Rico and go home," she pleaded.

"I am home," I told her and she hung up the phone in my ear. I know she is mad at me right now, but eventually she will come around. She will get tired of living like the Evans family sooner or later.

I took advantage of the fact that Milk was locked up to not only get close to Sabrina again, but to seize the opportunity to take over the streets he once ruled. I know I was the last person he ever expected to see again.

Daddy Daycare!

With no chrome on me to defend myself and all the muscle Byrd had around him, there wasn't a damn thing I could do when I saw the nigga. I was outnumbered, and for the first time in my life I felt like I had been defeated. I never left the house that night either. I got halfway to the door and realized I really had no place to go for real. Before I got locked up, when me and Sabrina would get into it I could hop in my truck and go on about my business until I cooled off enough to go back home. I wasn't about to go back into the bedroom and ask Sabrina if I could drive Juju's car, so I went in the room and got in the bed with Mj.

The only thing that kept me from going the fuck off was I really didn't have any proof that she was fucking with the nigga again like I did when I saw the pictures of her with Byrd. However, I have started checking her cellphone and going through her purse when she is sleep and that's some shit I never did before. She claimed to have a job interview this morning, one that she got through that Workforce shit she is in, and every second that she is gone I can't help but think that she could possibly be with Byrd.

I was tired of being cooped up in that tight ass apartment, so I took the kids outside to the park so

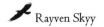

we all could get some fresh air. One thing about Carriage House is that even though it is considered a hood, because it was in Virginia Beach and funded by the city, it was a well maintained hood. I don't take them to the park too often though because Sabrina is not supposed to have anybody staying with her or she could get put out. Plus, I didn't fuck with none of the crabs in the bucket, in other words fake ass niggas who lived in the neighborhood either with their baby momma or girlfriends. It killed me to see niggas who once used to get dope from me getting money while I sat around being a house nigga.

"Look at me, Daddy," Saysha said.

"Daddy is looking at you, baby. Come on down."

"Daddy, you slide!" She ran over to where I was sitting on the bench holding Mj, who was sucking on his pacifier harder than Maggie Simpson, once she reached the bottom of the slide.

"Daddy too big to slide down. You go 'head and slide down for me. Give me a kiss before you go." Saysha climbed up on the bench, gave me a kiss, and then started jumping up and down. "Stop before you fall," I told her.

"I not gon' fall," she said, continuing to jump. I see she has a hearing problem just like her momma, so I plucked her on her thigh. She stopped jumping and just stood there looking at me.

"I told you to stop, didn't I?"

Saysha's eyes were starting to tear up. "Yes," she said, barely above a whisper. She nodded her head and a tear escaped out of the corner of her eye.

"Well, when Daddy tell you to do something, you listen. You hear me?" I was already starting to feel bad for plucking her but she has to learn how to listen. Sabrina can't do shit with her ass and I saw that when I first came home. All that falling out and shit I'm not going to have it.

"Yes." She nodded her head again.

I could see that she wasn't going to be able to hold those tears in much longer, and when she saw Sabrina walking up the side walk she jumped down off the bench and took off running towards her.

"What's the matter with my punkin'?" Sabrina bent down, scooped Saysha up in her arms, and then shifted her to her right hip. "What are you crying for?" She wiped Saysha's face.

"He hit me." Saysha pointed at me and leaned her head on Sabrina's chest.

"Don't say *he* hit you, Tell her yo' Daddy hit you," I sternly said, correcting her. It may take me some time but I'm going to break her little ass.
"What did you hit her for?" Sabrina asked me.

"There you go with that shit again. First of all I didn't hit her grown ass, I plucked her . . . and don't question me when I discipline her. That's why she don't pay you no mind."

"Milk, I told you to stop doing that. You may think you are not plucking her hard, but you don't

know your own strength." She put Saysha down who was now trying to hide behind Sabrina's leg so I couldn't see her. When she did I really took notice of the dress she wore to her interview and the heels she had on. It looked like some shit you would get out of K-mart.

One thing about Sabrina is she used to stay fly at all times, from her hair follicles on the top of her head down to her shoes. Today was the first time she hasn't worn her hair in a ponytail either since I been home. Had I not made it rain in Forbidden City with the money the niggas gave me after I spotted Byrd, she would have had some money to buy herself something decent to wear and pay the light bill, too. I guess I let seeing Byrd fuck with me and I felt like I had something to prove, but these niggas out here know I'm broke for real.

"Go play on the swings, Saysha." Sabrina walked over, and sat down beside me on the bench. "Hey, Mj, how you doing today," Sabrina pinched his cheeks. "You want to come to me." She held out her arms and Mj went right to her. Sabrina kissed him on the same cheek she was just pinching, then turned him around and sat him down on her lap. "I got the job." She smiled. I looked away from her.

"Oh, yeah," I sat up, put my elbows on my knees, and folded my hands together.

"Yes, and I start next Monday." I never looked to see if she was as happy as she sounded. "Aren't you proud of me?" She nudged me with her elbow.

"This is the first job I have ever had Milk, can you believe that?" *'Yeah I can believe it because I've always taken care of you,'* is what I was thinking.

"Well that's two of us that never had a job." I glanced over at Saysha as she climbed on top of the slide and was now trying to stand up. "Lil' girl," I called out to her. Saysha took one look at me and immediately started to climb down. "Come on and let's go in the house 'cause I see you trying me today. Come on." I stood up and took Mj off of Sabrina's lap. "I need to change him."

"Milk?"

"What," I answered Sabrina without looking at her.

"Don't you want to hear about my new job?" she said with a smile on her face.

"You said you got the job, what else is there for me to hear? You got a job and I'm running Daddy Daycare," I said, starting to walk towards the apartment building.

"I'm getting ready to come inside, too. It's hot out here!" Sabrina picked up Saysha and followed me.

I opened the door to the hallway and Tonikia was coming out the door at the same time. I don't know if she spent this much time at the girl's crib that lived upstairs from Sabrina, but I am starting to see her every day now. "My bad," I told her, taking a step back and holding the door open for her. Tonikia and Sabrina made eye contact with each other but neither one of them spoke. She

thanked me for holding the door open for her and kept walking.

Sabrina told me that she was going to take a shower and then she was going to make us some lunch. She probably been fucking and needed to wash the smell off. I told her that I had already fed the kids before I took them outside so they should be good for right now. Saysha started to perform for her momma again and acted like she hadn't eaten all day, so Sabrina gave her a Lunchables and told her to go sit at her Dora table and eat.

"Daddy, you want some?" she asked me. To be only two and a half years old Saysha was smart as shit and it amazed me how good she talked. She knew exactly what she was doing.

"Sit down and eat yo' food since you so hungry," I responded. She proudly smiled at me as if she knew what she had done. I swear she has been here before.

I changed Mj's pamper and gave him a bottle of apple juice. After he drank it down, he put his pacifier back in his mouth. Suddenly, there was somebody knocking at the door and Sabrina was still in the shower, so I put Mj down in his play pin and answered the door. *'Oh hell nawl!'* The last person I was in the mood for was Dancing Queen.

"How you doing, Milk?" Juju asked. I ignored him and left him standing at the front door. He was smiling too damn hard for me.

"Juju!" Saysha ran over to him and jumped into his arms.

"Well hey little Miss Diva in training! I miss you," he said, picking her up. "I brought you something." Juju put Saysha down and handed her a bag. She wasted no time rummaging through it.

"Oohhh . . . look, Daddy," Saysha said, holding up a pair of Dora pajama's with matching shoes.

"Tell 'em thank you," I told her.

"Thank you, Juju," she said, hugging him again.

"You're welcome." Juju smiled.

"My brother over there," Saysha pointed to Mj.

"I see . . . looking like a mini Milk." Juju looked at me but I turned my head the other way. "Where yo' momma at?"

"Right here," Sabrina said, walking back into the living room.

"Hey, bitch!" Juju stood up.

"Juju!" Sabrina looked at Saysha.

"Ooops . . ." He put his two fingers over his lips. "Sorry. I haven't been around chirren' since y'all moved out. Let me get a piece of Orbit gum for my dirty mouth so I can clean it up!" Juju and Sabrina started laughing. Just hearing the sound of his voice was starting to irk the shit out of me.

"So, bitch, did you get the job?"

"Juju!" Sabrina gave him a wide eyed look.

"Oh shoot, I did it again didn't I? I'm sorry. But did you get the job?"

"I got the job," Sabrina excitingly answered.

"Get it, bitch!" Juju hugged Sabrina again. She didn't say anything else to the faggot for cussing

again. "You know what you need to go with your new job?" He popped his lips.

"What?" Sabrina asked.

"A car," Juju answered.

"I know and I am going to try my best to get one as soon as possible. I really appreciate you letting me use your car for so long."

"That's not what I mean, love. You can have that car. Here go the registration right here already signed over to you." Juju reached into his man bag, took out the registration, and handed it to Sabrina.

"Are you serious?" Sabrina smiled at Juju. I couldn't believe how happy she was to be the owner of a 2006 Ford Taurus, but I guess when you don't have a car of your own a Pinto would excite you.

"Yes, I'm serious. Happy Birthday bitch!" I quickly looked at Sabrina. Today is her birthday.

'Damn!

Unemployed!

I was lying across the bed waiting for Milk to come into the bedroom, and I looked at the candles to make sure they were still burning. I could see the surprise on Milk's face when he opened the door. He turned the lights on.

"Don't just stand there. Come in and close the door."

"What's up?" he asked, sitting down on the side of the bed and taking his shoes off.

"I'm what's up! You don't like my outfit?" I got up off the bed and posed for him.

I didn't remind Milk that my birthday was coming up because I knew it would make him feel bad for not being able get me anything. He has been very distant for the last few days and gone more often than home. I was starting to get the feeling that he was hustling again. My Aunt Neicy sent me a gift card to Victoria's Secret for my birthday and I spent most of it on a red satin and lace teddy. Milk stood up and took his shirt off, but it seemed like he was trying to avoid looking at me.

"What's wrong with you, Milk?"

"Ain't nothing wrong. I'm 'bout to go take a shower," he answered, while walking around me as if I wasn't standing there half naked.

"Don't keep telling me there is nothing wrong. You're gone all the time now and when you are here you barely say two words to me."

"Not now, Sabrina," he said as he took off his pants.

"I don't want to hear that either. You ain't been home a good month. What you fucking somebody already?" I said with an attitude. Milk ignored me and opened the bedroom door, but I blocked him from leaving out of the room.

"Ain't nobody fucking nobody, now would you move?" Milk stood there and waited for me to move, and when I didn't he went back over to the bed and picked the jeans up off the floor that he just took off less than a minute ago.

"Where are you going now?" I closed the bedroom door. I didn't want to wake up the kids.

"Out," he said. After putting his boots on and lacing them up, he walked towards the door.

"Out where?" I folded my arms across my chest. Then I locked the bedroom door and stood in front of the door knob. Surprisingly Milk didn't put up a fight. Any other time he would have picked me up and moved me out the way but he didn't. Instead, he went back over to the bed and sat down. Then he ran his hands down his face in aggravation and stood right back up.

"I ain't fucking with nobody, Sabrina," he calmly said.

"Like you would admit to it if you were. I won't make you stay if here is not where you want to be."

I moved from in front of the door and walked over to the dresser.

"Where I want to be at then, prosecutor?" he asked in a sarcastic tone.

"No telling with you, Milk." I opened my top dresser drawer to get a t-shirt.

"Whatchu' doing, Sabrina?" he asked. I ignored him, put my t-shirt on, and started angrily blowing out the candles. "Stop blowing out the candles." Milk turned the lights back off. He walked up to me from behind because my back was still turned to him. "Turn around, Sabrina." I didn't move. "Oh, I forgot you and yo' daughter don't hear so good." I laughed even though I really didn't want to think about Saysha's bad ass right now. Milk turned me around to face him. "Get naked." I looked at him for a long, hard second because I remembered the last time he told me to get naked he acted a damn fool. He must have sensed what I was thinking because he started laughing. "I promise you will enjoy me telling you to get naked this time."

And this time he stayed true to his word. Milk put on me what I like to call the 'head to toe dick' because there was not one part of my body that he did not have in his mouth at some point. We did it in every position possible, and I think Milk even created new positions on his own. The way he put the loving on me I knew he wasn't cheating on me, or at least not yet anyway. I could always pin point when Milk was cheating because our sex would slack up in more ways than one. I used to tell him

that he was out there giving the good dick to the bitches in the street and saved the slum dick for me.

There was only one candle still lit and the room was a lot dimmer now, but I could still see Milk. He was staring at the ceiling with a look on his face like he had the weight of the world on his shoulders.

"Sabrina, this shit is driving me insane," he said in a low tone.

I knew my man, so I knew exactly what he was talking about. Now that I think about it that is the reason he has been walking around here like he has lost his mind. I've had over a year to adjust to our change in lifestyle, but I knew it was going to be harder for Milk to adapt to our new way of life once he came home.

"Milk, have you ever thought about everything that happened to us happened for a reason?" I sat up.

"Yeah, it happened for a reason, and the reason was 'cause of some snitching ass niggas!"

"I didn't mean it like that." I sat up. "Things could have been a lot worse than the sentence you received. I don't want you to ever go to jail and have to leave us again. We have kids now and they come first."

"You right, they do come first and right now I can't do a damn thing for them," Milk quickly responded. "And lay back down. You start to get loud when you're sitting up."

"No I don't," I said, laying back down and putting my arm across his chest.

"Trust me, you do," Milk said, pulling me closer to him.

"Milk, we're not in our twenties anymore."

"I know that Sabrina, but what does that have to do with anything?" He looked down at me.

"All I'm saying is that I don't want you to do anything that will jeopardize you losing your freedom again, or mine either for that matter. Milk, do you realize that you have some years hanging on your head?"

"I know that, too."

"Well to me it is not worth it. Not the money, the cars, or jewelry . . . none of that shit is worth going through what we just went through."

"So whatchu' gon' do, get me a job down there where you work at?" Milk went back to using that smart tone again. I didn't say anything. "What I'm supposed to do? Go down to the unemployment office and tell them I have been recently unemployed? Or better yet, let me check the want ads and see if they are hiring anywhere for brain surgeons, and if so, I will be the first to apply!"

"Don't be funny." I plucked him just like he plucks Saysha.

"No, don't you be funny. You know how fucked up I feel that not only did I forget yo' birthday, but had I remembered won't shit I could do or give you."

"You coming home was my birthday present," I softly said, feeling Milk's frustration of not being able to provide for his family.

"Bae, that's all well and good but what is the point of me being here when I can't pay that light bill that's been on the refrigerator since I've been home?"

"Don't worry about that light bill. I have already been approved for fuel assistance and by the time they send another bill it should be credited to my account."

"Call it what it is, a cut off notice."

"Milk, the lights are not going to get cut off."

"I know. You 'bout to start yo' new job and take care of all of us."

"What is that supposed to mean?" I sat up again. "Milk you have been taking care of me for a long time. Let me hold things down for right now until we figure something out." Milk sighed.

"Just leave it alone, Sabrina. Lift up," he said, taking his arm from around me. Milk turned over in the bed and I was now looking at the back of his head. I knew what that meant, he was through talking.

Forbidden City!

Anybody driving past Forbidden City before the remodel might have looked at the club as nothing more than a neighborhood juke joint, but the first time I drove past it I saw opportunity. If I was going to attempt a takeover I had to get my ducks in a row. Gremlin was my eyes and ears when we first came up to Virginia because I really didn't know my way around the area. Other than Virginia Beach, the remaining six out of the seven cities weren't in my travel path. I needed to find out who the players out here were since Milk was locked up, and where else do you find niggas gathered in a public setting other than the barbershop? A strip club!

I became a regular customer at Forbidden City and after a month of frequenting the club I offered Fox, the owner, an offer he could not refuse. Needless to say I own the club now, but I told Fox to keep the business in his name. Plus, he gets a weekly salary to manage it. I also spent a great deal of time at Forbidden so I could peep out signs of new money, and that's when I took notice of Onion.

I used to sit in my office and watch him from the time he pulled up in the parking lot to the time he made his way inside the club. I had cameras installed inside and outside when I remolded. The

way the dancers flocked to him when he came into the club was an indication to me that he was a big spender with the ladies. He popped bottles all night and a few times he bought out the bar. He was flashy with the ice he wore and there were always niggas swarming around him, so he automatically became a person of interest.

When I told Sabrina that I had left town and came back I was actually telling her the truth. I had to make a trip further up north to find the Angreos family. My granddad introduced me to Paulie Angreos when the time came for him to back away from the streets and pass the business down to me. At the same time Chino, Paulie's first born son, was also beginning to take a more active role in the New York family. When I arrived in New York, I found out that Chino and several other capos in the Angreos family were in federal prison on racketeering and drug charges. I put Gremlin on to Chino so I'm sure his going to prison was the reason Gremlin reached out to Milk for some dope, unaware that he was on to him.

One thing about Italians is that they don't want mulignan, as they called black people, fucking with their daughters, but if your money is right they will do business with you. The more you buy the less you pay for the product, and it made it easier to sway the niggas in the area my way with my new found friend, Onion, of course. Now with a place to receive my weekly re-ups and muscle to hold down the streets the only thing left to do was sit back and wait for Milk to come home. My last task in completing the ultimate low key take over was to obtain something else, or should I someone else, who I deemed as mine and that was Sabrina. Yeah, I did get me some pussy here and there, but shit, sex is easy to get and real love is hard to find.

"Yo', Byrd, you back here man?" Onion knocked on my office door.

"Hold up a second," I told him. I started to gather up the money I was counting and put it in the safe behind the mini bar. I picked my gun up off the table, tucked it in my back, walked over to the door, and opened it. "Y'all come on in." I walked over to the black, leather couch that took up most of the space in the room and sat down.

"What's going on?" Maine walked in behind Onion and walked over to me to shake my hand.

"I can't call it. You ready to get money, nigga?" I slapped hands with him.

"All day long and twice on Saturday," Maine answered, sitting down in a chair across from me.

"Yo', Onion, let me holla' at Maine for a minute, man."

"A'ight, I'll be at the bar." I waited for him to close the door before I spoke to Maine again. "You know me and that nigga you came up in here with that night got beef, don't you?" I got up off the couch and walked over to the mini bar to pour me a drink.

"Who, Milk?"

"Yeah, Milk," I said, trying to feel him out.

"Shit, man, I didn't even know you knew Milk. He ain't say shit to me 'bout no beef with you," Maine said, sitting up in the chair.

"Well, we do and he ain't welcome in my club no more." I sat back down on the chair and took a swig of my drink.

"Hold up, man!" Maine stood up. "Look, that's my nigga. I don't know what y'all got going on, but it must not be that serious or he would have told me."

"Have a seat," I told him, guzzling down the rest of my drink. "My beef is with him, not you." I sat the empty glass down on the table and Maine sat back down. "I'mma' still put you on to the raw and at a real good price, too, but Milk can't get so much as a tablespoon of the dope that I sell to you."

"Look, man, I know you not from around these parts but Milk ain't no nigga to sleep on. Now, like I said," he stood up again, "the nigga ain't said shit to me 'bout you. I'm just trying to eat. If we gon' do business, let's do business."

"I know the nigga ain't nothing to sleep on and I also know that he ain't gon' just let shit be between me and him. All I'm saying is there may come a time when you have to choose a side. I may be new to the area, but I ain't new to the game and your boy is done. He won't make a nickel in these streets as long as I am around... and I don't plan on going nowhere no time soon."

I Spy!

Milk may not be too thrilled about my new job, but I look forward to getting up every day and going to it. It feels good to be making my own money, plus I really enjoy what I am doing. I am getting a lot of hands on training when it comes to interior design as an assistant and the work experience will enhance my resume. I haven't told Milk yet, but I do plan to go back to school to finally complete the Interior Design/Architecture program and receive my degree.

Juju was right when he said that I was too dependent on Milk. Stephanie used to say that the only reason I stayed with him was because I was too afraid to stand on my own feet, and to some degree I guess it was true. My momma did the best she could to take care of me and Stephanie growing up, but we had some trying times and I never wanted to struggle like that again. I realized once Milk went to prison that I could make it on my own, even with a child.

Social services wasted no time cutting off my food stamps and monthly TANF check. Had I not gotten the job through The View program I would have just let the six months run out and not recertified when the time came, but my worker was on it. She spread the news to my section eight

worker and my rent went from zero to four hundred and twenty dollars in a matter of seconds, but if it means that I don't have to deal with folks all up in my business from social services then so be it. They served their purpose and I had no intentions of staying on welfare for the rest of my life anyway. For now, I just have to do what I have to do until do gets better.

I stopped at Food Lion on my way home from work today to pick up a few things, and as I was standing in line to pay for the groceries I saw Yvette and the white girl Jennifer, her partner in crime, walk into the store. Yvette was carrying a tote bag and Jennifer was wearing a long coat in the middle of summer, so it didn't take a rocket scientist to figure out that they came into the store to steal. I quickly turned my head the other way because I didn't want her to see me. Food Lion was right across the street from Carriage House and I didn't want her to find out which apartment was mine and tell Rico. I'm sure Yvette was still his go to person when he wanted to know something about me.

I keep my cell phone turned off most of the time because I never knew when Rico was going to call or send me a text message. I woke up one morning and my cell phone was on the floor beside my bed instead of in my purse where I left it the night before. Saysha is always going in my purse in search of candy and she may have had it, but I have the feeling it was her daddy playing "I Spy" so now I keep my phone locked.

I'm starting to notice certain things about Mj. Saysha was playing with him the other night, well trying to anyway, but nothing seems to interest him. In fact, he rarely makes eye contact with anybody, nor does he babble, make other baby noises, or respond to you when his name is called. As far as I know Nicole still has not called Milk to check on him, but as his momma I know she has to have noticed these things herself. It is bitches like her that give mothers a bad name.

When it Rains it Pours!

"Come on man, what's wrong with you today?" I patted Mj on his back as I walked him around the living room in my arms trying to get him to stop crying.

"Daddy, I can't hear TV," Saysha whined. I know the crying was getting on her nerves because he has been crying damn near all day.

"Mj don't feel good today, baby." I picked his bottle up off the counter and sat down on the couch to feed him, but he ain't want that either.

"He a crybaby," grown ass said. "He want his momma." I started laughing. I took that to mean Saysha was ready for him to go home.

"How you know what he want lil' girl?" Just then Sabrina walked in the house carrying two grocery bags.

"Mommy..." Saysha ran over to her.

"Hey punkin', what have you been doing today?" she asked her. "What's wrong with him, Milk? I heard him crying as soon as I walked into the hallway." She walked into the kitchen, sat the bags down on the counter, and walked back into the living room.

"I don't know." I shook my head. "This nigga been crying all day."

"What's the matter?" Sabrina said, taking him out of my arms. Mj immediately stopped crying as if he had been waiting for her to come home.

"Ain't this some shit?" I looked at up at Mj. Sabrina sat down next to me on the couch.

"You just don't know what to do for him, ain't that right?" Sabrina kissed him on his cheek.

"Don't get too comfortable laying up on her chest nigga. Get yo' own woman," I seriously told him, letting out a chuckle and going into the kitchen to put the food away.

"Mommy, can you play wit' me?" Saysha climbed up on the sofa and sat down next to Sabrina.

"In a little while baby, okay?" I looked over at Saysha and I could tell that she was about to pick up where Mj left off with the crying. She was used to having all of Sabrina's attention, and now that Mj was here I knew she was a little jealous.

"Come on over here and help Daddy put the food up, Saysha," I said, trying to take her mind off not having Sabrina's attention.

"Okay," she happily said, jumping down off the sofa and running into the kitchen.

"What I tell you 'bout running in the house? Here you go." I passed her the juice boxes so she could put them in the refrigerator.

"Don't run," she said, as she put the juices on the shelf.

"A'ight then." I looked over at Mj and he was slowly falling asleep in Sabrina's arms. I guess he

was tired with all the crying he been doing. Sabrina waited a few more minutes before she got up and laid him down in his play pen.

"Dats' it, Daddy?" Saysha asked.

"Yeah, baby," I answered, closing the refrigerator door. Saysha went back over and sat down in her chair to watch TV and I followed Sabrina into the bedroom.

"How was work today?" I sat down on the bed and watched as she started to take her clothes off.

"It was good. We staged three houses today," she tiredly said, unbuttoning her shirt.

"Oh, yeah," I said dryly.

"Yes, and my feet are killing me." She sat down on the bed beside me. "Milk, I want to talk to you about something."

"What I do?" I looked at Sabrina.

"Nothing I hope. It's about Mj."

"What's wrong? You ready for him to go home, too?"

"No." She shook her head. "Why would you say that?"

"I just figured you were," I answered.

"I told you I don't have a problem with your son being here, but have you noticed that he is not talking at all?"

"Whatchu' mean?"

"I'm not trying to compare him to Saysha, but he should be more advanced than he is now. Kids usually start to say mama or dada around the age of six months. Mj is not talking at all and he is not walking either," she said with a concerned tone, while unzipping her skirt and taking it off.

"Some kids develop faster than others," I sharply responded. I was starting to get a little pissed off. Ain't shit wrong with my son.

"No, Milk." Sabrina shook her head. "I don't think that's it. Something isn't right. You might need to talk to his momma and take him to his pediatrician."

"Oh, so that's what this is about, Nicole?" I stood up. "Sabrina if you want him to go home that's all you have to say," I said, raising my voice.

"Wait a got damn minute." She raised hers, too. "This ain't got shit to do with Nicole and I don't appreciate you implying that. I treat Mj no different than I do Saysha so you can kill that noise." I saw Saysha standing in the hallway.

"What's wrong Saysha?" I asked her and she walked into the room.

"I want my mommy," she said.

"Mommy and Daddy talking right now," Sabrina told her. Saysha had her hands behind her back.

"Come here Saysha." I called.

She walked into the room with her hands still behind her back but I could see she was holding something.

"Mommy, can I have some of dis' candy?" She held up a box.

'What the fuck!' I looked at Sabrina.

"What did I tell you about going in my pocketbook?" Sabrina snatched the box from her.

"Go in there and sit down." Saysha started crying and ran out of the room.

"Whatchu' doing with that?" I pointed to the EPT pregnancy test that Saysha took out of her purse.

"Don't get alarmed. I'm just a few days late."

"And you won't gon' say shit to me about it?" I got up and closed the bedroom door.

"I don't know if there is anything to say. I haven't taken the test yet, Milk."

"Well, ain't no time like the present," I suggested.

I sat back down on the bed and waited for Sabrina to come out of the bathroom. I always wanted to have a house full of kids, but not right now. Not while I'm fucked up like this. Five minutes later I heard the bathroom door open. Sabrina walked into the room and stood at the bedroom door. I could tell by the look on her face that it was going to be an addition to Daddy's daycare. *'Fuck!'*

I got up again and walked past Sabrina, went into the living room, and sat down. Sabrina's cellphone was ringing but I didn't see it anywhere. I stood up to check and see if I was sitting on it because I wanted to see who was calling her.

"Daddy . . . mommy phone ringing," Saysha said, holding it up in the air.

"Stay out yo' momma pocketbook, you hear me?" I looked at the phone while pretending to scold her and saw that it was Ms. Janis calling. "Go give the phone to yo' momma."

"Okay," she said, taking off running.

"Stop running," I told her, sitting back down on the couch.

When I heard Sabrina scream I jumped up off the couch and ran into the bedroom. Sabrina was on her knees crying and her cell phone was on the floor next to her. Saysha had started crying, too, after seeing how upset her momma was. I asked Sabrina what was wrong and when she didn't answer me I picked the phone up to talk to Ms. Janis. She told me that Sabrina's daddy passed away this morning. Damn, when it rains it pours!

Family Secrets!

I walked into my momma's house and closed the front door behind me. I went into the kitchen, sat my purse down on the table, and when I turned around my momma was walking towards me with her arms outstretched.

"I can't believe he is dead, Ma!"

"I know, baby," she said, holding me tightly in her arms. "He's in a better place now." I was still in my momma's embrace when my sister Stephanie walked into the kitchen. I could tell that she had been crying, too, because her eyes were red and swollen. I let go of my momma and we both sat down at the table.

"You alright, baby?" my momma asked Stephanie who shook her head no.

I reached over and grabbed a napkin from the napkin holder that was centered in the middle of table and wiped my eyes with it. "So where do we start?" I looked at Stephanie.

"What do you mean where do we start?" Stephanie had a look of disgust on her face. "Everything is pretty much taken care of." She folded her arms across her chest.

"What do you mean everything is taken care of? Dad died this morning." I looked at my momma and then back to my sister.

"Sabrina, you know how your father was. He was very meticulous when it came to certain things and he left no stones unturned," my momma pointed out.

"So what are you saying?" I asked my momma. At this point I was confused.

"You don't have to worry yourself with funeral arrangements and all that. I will handle everything," Stephanie said.

"What do you mean I don't have to worry about the funeral arrangements? He was my father, too!" I stood up.

"Umph . . ." Stephanie pressed her lips together and turned her head.

"What the fuck is that supposed to mean, Stephanie?"

"You two don't start," my momma stood up, "now is not the time." She held up both of her hands.

"It's not like you have any money to pay for anything." Stephanie ignored what my momma had just told us and stood up, too. "I'm sure you're busy with the baby, jail visits, and all of that," she said, voice trailing off at the end.

"Kiss my ass, Stephanie!"

"Lord Jesus!" My momma looked up to the ceiling. "Look now, you both are upset and now is not the time for you two to being going at it!"

"Goodbye, Mother!" Stephanie put on her coat. "I have a lot to do in the morning and I don't have

time for any of Sabrina's mess tonight." I followed my sister to the front door.

"You know what, Stephanie," I raised my voice, "I accept the fact that you and I can't get along for whatever reason, but you would think that this would be the one time that we came together for daddy's sake." Stephanie turned around.

"When is the last time you even talked to him?" she asked. "When is the last time you went to visit him?"

"You know what? Never mind . . . go on about your business, Stephanie, because I already see where this is going." I left my sister standing at the front door but she quickly followed me back into the kitchen.

"No," she said, walking behind me. "Answer my question!"

"Leave it alone, Stephanie," my momma said, raising her voice. Stephanie looked at my momma.

"What you really mean is leave Sabrina alone. Right?"

You heard what I said," my momma sternly answered. I was looking at the eye contact Stephanie and my momma were making with each other.

"Why of course I did," Stephanie said in a sarcastic tone. "We can't upset Princess Sabrina, now can we?"

"Don't make me have to say it again," my momma said with her eyebrow raised.

"Oh, I heard you!" Stephanie sternly looked at my momma and then to me.

"Look," I snapped. "All I want to do is make sure that my father's home going is right. That's all. This is not about you and it's not about me!"

"Now that is the one thing you got right today. This is not about you!" Stephanie shifted her purse from her hand to her shoulder.

"Stephanie," my momma calmly said. "I mean it."

"Stop with all the subliminal messages. If you got something you want to say to me, then just say it!" I folded my arms across my chest.

"Trust me . . . I could say a whole lot right now."

"Well say it then, bitch!" I said, walking towards my sister.

My momma stepped in between both us and put her hands up as if she were a boxing referee. "I'm not having this shit tonight and I mean it," she said.

"Mother, why don't you just be honest and tell her the truth! I'm tired of all the family secrets," Stephanie yelled.

"Tell me the truth about what? What family secret?" I yelled back.

"Stephanie, be quiet!" My momma was now yelling, too.

"I will not be quiet!" she fired back. "Somebody should have told her a long time ago!"

"Told me what?" I looked at my momma.

"Go ahead, Mother. Tell her!"

"Tell me what, Ma?" I looked at my momma and lowered my voice.

"Nothing, baby, Stephanie . . ." she looked at my sister.

"Sabrina, you are adopted," Stephanie blurted out.

"What?" I frowned up my face. I looked at my momma and she had her head down. "Ma?" she looked up at me but she didn't say anything. "Is that true?"

"Yes, it's true," Stephanie answered for her. "You always wondered why Asia and I were so close. Well, now you know. She was my blood . . . and I'm sure you know how the saying goes."

Look Daddy!

Sabrina didn't go to her daddy's funeral nor was she speaking to anybody in her family, except Juju. I could never bring myself to tell Sabrina that I had known for a long time that she was adopted. Asia told me that years ago, but I felt as if it wasn't my place to tell Sabrina if Ms. Janis didn't want her to know for whatever reason. I did call Stephanie and cussed her ass out though. Now was not the time for her to put that out there like she did as if their daddy's passing wasn't enough to deal with.

I hate to see my baby hurting like this especially when there's nothing I can do to fix the situation. I'm sure the stress of everything that is going on was the reason she had a miscarriage. Now that's another loss she has to deal with, but to be honest it was somewhat of a relief to me that we were not going to have another baby right now.

"Daddy, can I go in da' room wit' mommy?" Saysha asked me.

"Naw, let mommy sleep," I told her, while sitting her on my lap.

"When her gon' get up, Daddy?"

"When she feels better, baby." I kissed her on the forehead.

"Go peek yo' head in the room and see if yo' brother is still asleep."

"Okay," she said, hopping down off my lap and running off.

"Saysha . . ."

"Me know, stop running." I laughed to myself. That little girl is terrible. I started flipping through the TV channels with the hope of catching a basketball game. "Him still sleep, Daddy," she said, climbing back up on my lap. "Can I turn the TV?"

Saysha has just learned how to turn the TV channels with the remote and she has become fascinated with it. I guess this will be another night of The Disney Channel.

"Here you go." I gave her the remote and sat her down next to me on the couch.

I've been thinking about what Sabrina told me about Mj and I am starting to see what she is talking about. When I talked to Nicole about it she said the same thing that I told Sabrina that some kids develop faster than others, but I'm convinced it's more to it than that. I told her to call his pediatrician and make an appointment for one day next week and I would meet her there.

"Daddy be right back, okay?" I told Saysha.

"Okay," she answered, keeping her attention focused on the TV. I got up and went in the room to check on Sabrina.

"Bae, can I get you anything?" I laid down on the bed next to Sabrina and put my arm around her as she shook her head no. "Bae, you have to get up and eat something," I softly said.

"I don't want anything to eat," she responded, pulling the covers up around her neck.

"When are you going to talk to yo' momma, Sabrina," I asked, drawing her closer to me.

"Milk, will you leave me alone?"

"No, I'm not gon' leave you alone, Bae. You gotta' talk yo' momma sooner or later."

"No, I don't. I don't want to talk to nobody." She moved over to the other side of the bed away from me.

"Sabrina . . ." I sat up in the bed.

"Milk, leave me alone," she hollered.

"Bae, calm down, I'm not trying to upset you," I said, trying to soothe her. "But you being adopted doesn't change who yo' momma and daddy have been to you. You know that you are Ms. Janis' heart and she loves you very much." I waited for Sabrina to respond but she didn't. When I saw her body trembling I knew that she was crying. I laid back down beside her and put my arm back around her, but I didn't say anything else. I just held her in my arms and let her have her cry until she fell asleep.

"Daddy . . . Daddy . . . look!" Saysha yelled from the other room. I eased my arm from up under Sabrina and got up to go see what she was so excited about. "Look, Daddy . . . its Maine," she said, pointing to the TV.

"Let me see this!" I took the remote away from Saysha, sat down beside her on the couch, and turned up the volume on the TV.

". . . the victim was found shot to death early this morning and has now been identified as Tremaine Redden. As of now the police have no suspects in custody related to this shooting. If you have any information that would assist the Portsmouth Police Department in this investigation, you are asked to call 1-889-LOCKUUP. John, back to you. . ."

Riches before Bitches!

Instead of being a hairstylist, Janea should have gone to school for broadcast journalism because she could report the local news just as good as the people on the six o'clock news. She stays up on current events, and by her latest report Maine was found shot to death on a school bus. The last time I saw Maine was when he came to the house with Milk after I shot that intruder. I hoped that this was an isolated incident and there wasn't anybody trying to kill my baby daddy. I don't think Sabrina can handle two kids on her own, especially one who is retarded.

Mj's pediatrician told me six months ago that he needed to be seen by a child development specialist right after his hearing test came back normal. She said Mj was not meeting the milestones for his age and she suspected there may be a problem. I never took Mj back to see her or a developmental specialist either for that matter. I didn't have time for all of that shit; if he is retarded he's retarded. What is there for a specialist to do? I just needed somebody to give him his shots when I brought him in for a visit and then send us on our way. If Milk wants to deal with it then he can have at it. Just leave me out of it!

I did tell him that I would make the appointment for him but I didn't tell him I was going to the doctor with him, and besides, I have better things to do with my time. Me and my new BFF Angelle are picking out some curtains to go with the furniture her boyfriend, Onion, just brought for their new house. I know—tedious ain't it? But a girl gotta' do what a girl's gotta' do to get in close proximity when plotting to take someone's man. I just hope she takes it well.

I don't rock with any other chicks around here and I do actually like Angelle. She was in the delivery room with me when I had Mj and even brought me home from the hospital. She also helped me find a daycare for him, so I guess me fucking with her man will have a definite impact on our friendship. I believe in riches before bitches, and Angelle should look at it as a down payment on some common sense for being so trusting of people.

Me and My God!

Singing . . .

". . .don't forget me, I beg . . . I remember you said . . . Sometimes it lasts in love but sometimes it hurts instead . . . Sometimes it lasts in love but sometimes it hurts instead. . ."

I turned off the bathroom light, closed the door behind me, and followed the sound of the music that was playing. "What's up?" I spoke to Sabrina when I walked past the kitchen.

"Good morning," she responded. "How are you feeling?"

"Can you turn that down some? I got a headache."

"Oh, I'm sorry. Juju got me hooked on this CD. Did it wake you up?" She reached over and turned the volume down on the radio.

"Did it wake me up? Shit, I ain't been to sleep," I thought to myself. I looked over to see what Sabrina was cooking and immediately lost my appetite. "I know them kids sick of fucking Oodles and Noodles." Sabrina looked at me and rolled her eyes. "You can roll yo' damn eyes all you want. I don't care how many different flavors they have, all them shits taste the same!" Sabrina mumbled

something under her breath but I couldn't understand what she was saying. "Let me shut the fuck up," I said, going into the living room and sitting down. "Broke niggas don't have a voice."

"I ate noodles growing up and I survived. Besides, they don't eat them every day so stop it. I'm going to make groceries when I get paid on Friday."

"Whatchu' trying to say," I stood up and walked back over to the kitchen.

"I'm not trying to say anything, Milk. Damn!" she said, slamming the spoon she was using to stir the food with on the counter.

"You don't have to keep throwing the fact that you have a job in my face. Who the fuck cares!"

"Milk leave me the alone. I don't feel like arguing with you today."

"Ain't nobody arguing with you, Ms. Independent. I see you." I smiled at Sabrina.

"Milk . . ."

I don't know what Sabrina was about to say but whatever it was it was interrupted when the lights shut off. You would think we were having a moment of silence as quiet as it was in the apartment, but when I heard the music coming from the apartment upstairs I knew that there wasn't a power outage. The mothafuckin' lights had been turned off!

"Daddy . . ." Saysha ran into the living room yelling, "My TV broke!" She whined and then started crying. "Daddy, can you fix it?" I looked over at Sabrina. *"Daddy can't fix shit,"* I thought to myself.

"Come here, Saysha," Sabrina called out to her. I walked past Sabrina who was now holding Saysha and went in the room, put my shoes on, and left the house.

I was mad, ashamed, enraged, embarrassed and some more shit, and right now I felt like less than a man. I don't cry that often, but when I do it's just between me and my God.

Sleeping Bears!

I had to pull myself together and get out of bed. The initial shook of everything had worn off, but I was still trying to make sense of it all. I just didn't understand why my momma didn't tell me when I was younger that I was adopted. It would not have made me love her or daddy any less had I known the truth. Once again, I'm feeling like the biggest fool and as always I'm the last to know. Milk has been as supportive as he knows how to be, but even if he had the money there was nothing in this world that he could buy me that could make me feel better.

With everything that had been going on I forgot about the extension I had put on the light bill. I had the money. I just had to go pay the bill and the lights were turned back on within two hours. Milk still had not come home and he hadn't called me since he left this morning. I was really starting to worry about him. He took Maine's death just as hard as he did Kirk's and I was praying Rico didn't have anything to do with it. This could be the very thing to set Milk off and send him on a rampage. Some people just don't know when to let sleeping bears lie.

"Mommy, can I wash my baby hair?"

"You can when you take a bath. Now hold your head back before you get water in your eyes," I told Saysha softly, rinsing the shampoo out of her hair.

"Where my Daddy go?"

"I don't know, baby." I turned the water off and reached for a towel. "Sit up," I said, while wrapping the towel around her head.

"Okay," she replied. I helped her get down off of the counter and she ran over to Mj who was sitting in the walker that I bought for him. "Mommy . . . Mj stink!" Saysha said, while pinching her nose.

I walked into the living room. "Ummm . . . he do don't he?" I took Mj out of the walker and laid him down on the couch. "Saysha, pass mommy Mj's wipes."

"Where?" She looked around.

"Right there." I said, pointing. Saysha got the wipes and brought them to me.

"Mommy, why Mj don't have a *tt* down 'der," she pointed between her legs, "like me?"

"Because Mj is a little boy and you are a little girl. That's why," I answered my inquisitive daughter.

"Mj's *tt* looks like a French fry," she said, starting to laugh. I couldn't help but to laugh, too.

"Don't worry about your brother's French fry. Go in your room and get your hair box off the dresser with your bows in it so I can finish your hair after I change Mj."

I got Mj squared away and Saysha still had not come back in the living room with her hair box.

"You see it, Saysha?"

"I'm using the 'bafroom, Mommy," she called out from the bathroom.

"Okay."

My cell phone was on the couch next to me and I noticed a flashing red light indicating that I had a new text message, and when I looked to see who it was from I rolled my eyes at the ceiling. It was from Rico and he had just sent the text to me two minutes ago.

"*I need to see you!*" the message said.

"Saysha, you okay in there?"

"Umm . . . hmm . . . my tummy hurt," she replied.

Since Milk knew I wasn't speaking to anyone in my family he didn't question me when I changed my phone number. I told Juju not to give it to anybody in our family but I failed to mention for him not to give it to Yvette either. Juju told me that he saw Yvette in the mall and she asked him for my new number, so he gave it to her.

"*I told you to stop texting me Rico,*" I typed and pressed send.

"*Meet me at the hotel in Hampton,*" was his response to my text.

"*I can't, Rico,*" I quickly replied and sent the message to him.

The next text message I received from Rico was my address and I took that to mean that if I didn't meet him in Hampton he would meet me at my house. Oh, I forgot to tell you that Juju gave Yvette my address, too.

"Lord, I don't need this right now," I said aloud to myself. I got up to go to the bathroom to check on Saysha who was too busy applying toothpaste to her hair and smearing it all over the counter in the bathroom to notice me standing there. "No wonder you so quiet in here. I'mma' beat your butt!"

First Blood!

Some people don't display good decision making skills when presented with a choice. I on the other hand look at the pros and cons of every situation before I decide on anything, especially when it comes to hustling. You have to or you will be the one fucked up in the end when it is all said and done. That's why I believe in giving people choices with the hopes that they would choose wisely. You see where I am going with this don't you?

I understood Maine's loyalty to Milk, and I also salute him for that because there are not too many niggas who hold high regard to that these days, but I really could give a fuck about Milk and Maine's allegiance to him! He may not be making any noise right now, but I know how Milk operates and I was going to be the one to draw first blood. Maine was just the first sacrificial lamb.

Memory Lane!

Selling the clothes that I stole was what I was doing as a source of income after Milk went to prison, but even without that money from boosting I would have still been okay with or without him. I believe in saving for a rainy day, unlike Sabrina. It's almost time to make another store run because my merchandise is starting to run low.

I was sitting on my bed counting the money I made today from the clothes I sold to some of the clients at the shop when I heard the doorbell ring. "I'm coming," I said aloud. I glanced at the time on the cable box and it was eight-thirty. *"Damn, he is early,"* I thought to myself. Onion was coming to see me tonight but he said around ten o'clock. I took one last look at myself in the full length mirror on the wall, dimmed the lights, and opened the front door.

"Dap?"

"Hey, Nicole, how are you doing?"

I reached my arms out to give him a hug. It had been almost a year since I saw or heard from him, and I have to admit I was happy to see him. "I'm fine. Where have you been?" I took a step back so that he could come inside. I turned the lights all the way up and closed the front door. "You can sit down."

"Where that boy at," Dap asked, looking around the room. I'm sure he was referring to Mj. He sat down on the couch and I sat down beside him.

"He's spending the night with Milk," I lied. *"He's doing more than just spending the night,"* I thought to myself.

"So, Milk is home, huh?" Dap put his head down.

"Yeah, he has been home for almost two months. You haven't seen him?" I asked.

"I'm sure I am the last person he wants to see." Dap rubbed his hands together.

"Why would you say that as close as you and Milk are?"

"Milk didn't tell you what I did?" He looked at me with his eyebrows pressed together.

"No," I shook my head. "He did ask me a few times had I heard from you when he first went to prison, but I told him I hadn't. I didn't know where you were. Did something happen between you two to make you leave town?" I could hear my cell phone chiming in the next room. "Wait a minute, that's my phone."

It was Onion calling to tell me that he was not going to be able to come see me tonight because he had some business to take care of. Being the patient person that I was, I told Onion that it was alright. He promised to make it up to me. I changed out of the dress I was wearing and put on something more comfortable.

"Can I get you anything?" I asked Dap, walking back into the living room.

"No, thank you. I'm alright," he answered. "Sit down, Nicole. I need to talk to you about something." Dap had his hands together again and was looking down at the floor. I sat down next to him.

"Talk to me about what? What's wrong?"

"Did Peaches ever tell you how we knew each other? How we met?" he asked, continuing to look down at the floor.

"I don't think so." I shook my head. "To tell you the truth, I never asked. I knew that Peaches lived here in Virginia for a while when she was younger. My grandma told me that when I was little. Why do you ask?" Dap let out a long sigh and then looked over to me.

"I meet your mother over thirty years ago. I had a barbershop up on Church Street that was next door to a corner store. I used to see Peaches all the time but I never said anything to her because I was married. Actually, I had two kids, too," he said. "But it was something about Peaches that I was drawn to. I couldn't wait to get to the shop every day with the hopes of seeing her." He shook his head and smiled. "One day on my way to the shop I told myself if I saw her I was going to say something to her, but I never got the chance to. Had I known the day before that I wouldn't see her again I would have approached her then. It was almost a year later when I did see Peaches again,

but it wasn't at the corner store. It was in a crack house."

"I really don't want to stroll down memory lane with you about your drug days with Peaches, Dap."

"Nicole, please. I've been carrying this around with me for too long." Dap had a sullen look on his face.

"Go ahead," I said, sitting back on the couch and letting out a sigh.

"When crack hit the seen back in the early eighties it changed a whole lot of people's lives and I wasn't excluded. I got caught out there and lost everything that I worked so hard for, along with my family, but I didn't care. As long as I had my drugs and Peaches I didn't need anything else, nor did I want anything else," he looked down at the floor and then back to me. "But then Peaches got pregnant."

"She got pregnant with who?" I wrinkled up my face.

"With you, Nicole," he said, starting to rub his hands together again.

"So what are you trying to say? Are you trying to tell me that you are my father?" I pointed to myself. Dap didn't respond. "Get out of my house!" I yelled. Then I quickly walked over to the front door and opened it. Dap stood up and walked over to me.

"Nicole, I'm sorry," he said. "I didn't tell you this now to hurt you."

"Hurt me?" I started laughing. "You didn't hurt me. I could care less. You're no different than Peaches."

"That's not true, Nicole. After Peaches found out she was pregnant with you she stopped getting high. It was me who couldn't leave the shit alone, and right before you turned one year old Peaches left Virginia and moved back to Florida with your grandmother, but a few months later she came back to Virginia by herself. Within a year she was pregnant again. I was in and out of jail back then and I lost contact with Peaches until years later."

"Why are you telling me all of this now?" I folded my arms across my chest.

"It was time you knew the truth, Nicole."

"Okay, so you told me. Now what?"

"I want to make things right with you, Nicole. You're my daughter," he said with sincerity in his voice.

"Didn't you say you and Peaches had another child? Go make things right with him. I don't have anything else to say."

"If I knew where she was," he lowered his head, "I would."

House Lady!

I closed the patio sliding door to Tonikia's apartment and looked around to see if anybody was standing outside. When I saw that the coast was clear I walked around to the front of the apartment building and went inside. I took my time closing the front door because I didn't want to make any noise or wake up Sabrina. I sat down on the couch, took off my shoes, and stretched out. No sooner than I closed my eyes every light in the house was on and Sabrina was standing over top of me.

"Milk, where have you been?" I started yawning.

"Whatchu' mean where have I been?"

"Don't try and act like you were in a deep sleep. I heard you when you came in," she said with conviction. I started laughing and sat up.

"I was just fucking with you, Bae," I said, getting up off the couch and going into the bedroom with Saysha's momma right behind me.

"You still have not answered my question." Sabrina closed the door behind her. "Where have you been?" When I took my jeans off my cell phone fell out of my pocket onto the floor. *Shit!* "And when did you get a cell phone?"

144

"Today," I answered, picking the phone up from off the floor and sitting it down on the dresser.

"For what? And where did you get money to buy a cell phone?" I wrinkled up my face at her.

"You got a cell phone don't you?"

"Where did you get the money to buy a cell phone, Milk?" She raised her voice.

"Sabrina, you are Saysha's momma, not mine. I don't know who the fuck you think you hollering at!"

"Look, Milk, I'm not putting up with none of your shit. You are not about to disrespect me in-" She must have thought about what she was about to say because she abruptly stopped talking.

"Go 'head and say it. I'm not about to disrespect you in yo' house. Ain't that what you were about to say?" Milk sarcastically asked.

"No, I-"

"Yes you was, Sabrina," I said, cutting her off again. "I guess 'get out' gon' be the next thing that come out yo' mouth, huh? My bad, house lady. For now on I will make sure I'm home before the street lights come on."

"Let me come in the house at five in the morning and it would be a fucking tragedy!" she said. "But since you want to start that bullshit, watch this."

"Watch what?" I walked over to Sabrina and got in her face. "What the fuck I need to watch?" I asked her through clenched teeth.

"Milk, get out of my face," she said, pushing me. I started to have more flashbacks of the pictures of Sabrina and Byrd together.

"I'm sure yo' ass had your share of late nights and early mornings when I was locked up." I walked past Sabrina to leave out of the bedroom. "What . . . you ain't got nothing to say now?"

"Milk, don't try and turn this around on me. The only thing open this time of night is 7-Eleven and legs and you still haven't told me where you have been." I opened the bedroom door.

"Where are you going?" Sabrina shouted.

"To take me a shower."

"What the bitch you were with don't have indoor plumbing?" Sabrina smirked.

"Man, leave me the fuck alone." I slammed the bathroom door shut, closed the lid on the toilet stool, sat down, and then buried my face in my hands.

I should have told Maine what was up with me and Byrd, but my pride wouldn't let me. I told him not to fuck with them niggas I just didn't tell him why. Sabrina once told me that if word ever got out in the street what went down between me and Byrd my name would be Mud instead of Milk, and even though she said it in the midst of an argument she was right. Now another one of my niggas is gone at the hands of that mothafucka'. Feds or no Feds, something has got to give.

Someone You Don't Meet Twice!

"Sabrina, it's me. Please don't hang up the phone."

"What do you want, Yvette?" I let out a long sigh.

"I know you probably hate me, Sabrina, and I'm sorry for what I did, but I really need your help," she pleaded.

"Don't call my phone again, Yvette." I said, hanging up before she had a chance to say anything else. Within a minute Yvette was calling my cell phone again. I didn't answer but I did end up calling her back after listening to the voicemail she left me. Even after everything she had done I still couldn't turn my back on her if she was in trouble.

We only had one house to stage today and I just so happened to have gotten off work early. I told Yvette I would come and pick her up only if she was going to let me take her to her momma's house and she agreed. I typed the address she gave me into the GPS on my phone and it directed me to the Great Bridge section of Chesapeake. When I turned into Cedar Creek Manor, I pulled over on the side of the road to check the address again. *"This can't be right,"* I said to myself, looking around the neighborhood. I have lived in Virginia

all of my life but I don't know my way around Chesapeake. I was expecting to see something similar to Ocean View, not houses with manicured lawns the size of the one Milk and I used to live in.

I drove up a little further until I reached the address Yvette told me she would be at. I blew the horn a couple of times, and when she didn't come out or answer her cell phone again when I tried calling her I decided to go knock on the door. When it opened I instantly regretted answering my phone for Yvette.

"Well, I couldn't come to you, so I had to bring you to me," Rico said.

"You know what? I'm about sick of you and Yvette." I looked around to see who may have been watching me.

"You have come all this way . . . you're not going to come in, Sabrina?"

"Yeah, I'mma' come in," I said, walking right past him inside of the house, "just long enough to cuss your ass out!" Rico closed the front door.

"Now why would you want to do that?" he said, trying to put his arms around me.

"Don't touch me, Rico," I said, pulling away from him. "You think this shit is funny don't you?"

"Not at all," he said from behind a smile bigger than a Cheshire cat's. "I'm just happy to see you!"

"What part of its over do you not understand?" I yelled.

"What do you think about the house? You like it?"

"Fuck this house and, and fuck you, too!"

"Come on, I'll give you a tour," he said. He tried to take me by the arm but I snatched away from him.

"I don't want a fucking tour, Rico. I just want you to leave me alone!"

"No you don't, Sabrina, 'cause if you really felt that way you would have told me to kick rocks when I showed up at your house that day."

"Had I known you were going to carry on like this I would have," I told him with feeling behind it.

"You cute when you mad. You know that?" Rico asked in a low tone.

"Rico, why are you doing this?"

"I love you, Sabrina. Don't you understand that by now? Whether you want to admit it or not, I know that you love me, too. What confuses me is why you still with the nigga in the first place. He can't do shit for you."

"What are your intentions, Rico?"

"To make you my wife one day, Sabrina," he said, pulling me closer to him.

"Rico . . ." I shook my head.

"Here me out, Sabrina," he said putting his hands on my shoulders. "What we had was real to me and I should not have let it go so easily. But now I'm willing to fight for you and there's nothing I won't do to make you mine. You're the kind of woman that you don't meet twice and I need you in my life. I bought this house for you and there is a car in the garage with the keys in the ignition." Rico

leaned down to kiss me but I pulled away from him.

"Rico, you are going to make some woman very happy one day, it's just not going to be me. I know you don't want to hear this but I love Milk and that's why I am with him."

"Sabrina, if that nigga didn't get shot you wouldn't be with him today. Tragedy always brings people together. You deserve the best of everything and that nigga ain't what it is. If you're worried about him doing something to you, if you leave him that should be the least of your worries. Milk is done in these streets. I saw to that." I looked at Rico like I was looking at a stranger.

"Did you have anything to do with Maine's murder?" I asked him even though I didn't expect him to tell me truth.

"I don't know anybody named Maine and you don't need to worry about what's going on in the streets."

"Is that right, Byrd?" Rico turned his head away from me. "What's wrong, I still can't call you that?"

"Have you been calling me that?" He looked at me sternly.

"I have to get home," I said, opening the front door again.

"I'm not going to give up on us, Sabrina." He walked up behind me.

"Let it go, Rico. Just let it go," I said, walking out of the door and closing it behind me.

Daddy Nobucks!

Milk popped up at my house un-expectantly this morning and dropped Mj off and it is really throwing a monkey wrench in my plans for today, or should I say for the weekend. Onion was going to take me to DC for a shopping extravaganza once he got back in town, so now I have to figure out something to do with his mentally challenged ass. I can't take him back to Angelle's cousin's daycare because then I really will have to hear Milk's mouth. I asked him when he was coming back to get his son, but all he said was that he would call me.

I just hope Milk is not neglecting his fatherly duties on the strength of Sabrina. She has absolutely no cause for complaints. I will continue to buy pampers, wipes, and anything else Rain Man, I mean Mj, may need. I almost want to throw a few dollars Milk's way. Shit, he used to own six barbershops and I'm sure somebody will give him a haircut and a face shave for free considering the current state of his finances. Milk went from Daddy Warbucks to Daddy Nobucks. If I see him wearing those same jeans one more time I'm going to go out and steal him a new pair!

Who Am I!

After I left Rico's house I stopped at the gas station to get some gas and a pack of cigarettes. I had been fighting the urge to smoke since I quit again but my will not to smoke has been depleted. Right now I think it is the only thing that may keep me sane. Before I knew it I had smoked three cigarettes by the time I made it home. I put two pieces of spearmint gum in my mouth before I got out of the car so Milk wouldn't smell the smoke on me. He has always hated the fact that I smoked cigarettes in the first place, and I didn't want to hear his mouth when I got in the house.

As I was walking up the sidewalk towards my apartment building, I saw what looked like two girls fighting, which was not uncommon to see out here in Carriage House. What shocked me was that the closer I got to the crowd of teenagers that formed around to cheer the fight on, was when I realized that one of them was my niece Aleeaha and she was wearing her opponent's ass out!

"Let her go, Aleeaha," I said, trying to break them apart. "Aleeaha, stop!" Now I know how Juju felt trying to break me and Nicole up. Aleeaha was strong. "Let her hair go, right now!" I was finally able to pull her off of the girl and made her go inside the apartment and I quickly followed behind her. "What the hell are you doing out here fighting?" I sat down on the couch to catch my breath. "Do you know I could get put out behind that mess? And what are you doing here in the first place?" I asked, bombarding her with questions.

"Aunt Sabrina, it wasn't my fault," she said, sitting down on the loveseat which was on the other side of the room.

"Mommy . . ." Saysha came running out of her room.

"Hey, punkin', stop running okay," I gave her a hug. "Go back in the room with Mj while I talk to Aleeaha."

"Him not here," she said. "He gone wit' my daddy," Saysha added. "Mommy, can you take me to da' park?"

"If you be a good girl and go back in your room to play I will take you later on."

"Okay!" She quickly smiled and ran back to her room.

"Aunt Sabrina, I was minding my own business taking out the trash when she came up to me and asked me where I was from like I needed her permission to be out here," she said, examining the scratches on her arm. "I should go back out there and beat her up again!"

"How did you get over here?" I asked her.

"Uncle Milk came to pick me up so I could watch Saysha for him. Aunt Sabrina, look," she held up her arm, "I think she bit me. I might need a rabies shot!"

"Milk came and picked you up with who?"

"He won't with nobody," she answered.

"Milk was driving?" Aleeaha shook her head yes. "What kind of car was he driving?" I asked. I waited for her to tell me it was a gold BMW so I could go the fuck off!

"He was driving a white van."

"*A white van,*" *I said to myself.* "Come over here and let me look at your arm," I said, calming down. Aleeaha got up and sat next to me on the couch.

"I hope I didn't get you in any trouble. Aunt Sabrina," she said.

"No, you did right. When somebody invades your space-" I paused when I realized I was about to tell Aleeaha the same thing my momma used to say to me and Stephanie growing up.

"You have the right to get them out of it," Aleeaha said, finishing my statement. "I know . . . Nana told me that, too." She started laughing.

"How is Nana?" I asked.

"She's alright, but I know she would be better if you called her?" I could tell by the look on her face that she knew something. "I overheard my momma and Nana talking about you."

"You did?" I asked.

She shook her head yes. "Aunt Sabrina, it doesn't matter to anybody that you were adopted. You're my aunt and I love you. The whole family does, even my momma, as crazy as she may act."

"Stephanie, loves me?" I pointed to myself. "Yeah, right!"

"Aunt Sabrina, why didn't you come to granddad's funeral?"

"I just couldn't." I shook my head. "Come on so I can take you home. Saysha," I called out to my daughter, but she didn't answer. "Saysha," I called again, but still no response. I got up off the couch and went in her room to see what she was doing. I stopped when I reached the door way to her bedroom, looked up at the ceiling, and said a silent prayer. "Saysha Aprea Woodhouse!"

"What she do, Aunt Sabrina?" Aleeaha asked looking over my shoulder. "Oohhh . . ." She put her hand on her mouth. "Don't beat her, Aunt Sabrina." She started laughing and Saysha started crying.

"I'm not. I never do, but she better be glad Milk isn't here. Come here so I can wash all that grease out of your hair." I looked around her room and there was hair grease all over the walls, comforter, table, and chairs. "Lord I will be glad when she is past her terrible two's. Come on here, lil' girl!"

"Aunt Sabrina, can I spend the night with you?" Aleeaha asked.

"You can spend the night next weekend," I told her. Any other time I wouldn't mind Aleeaha spending the night but I didn't want her to be here when Milk came home. He may have avoided my questions the night when he strolled his ass in here at five o'clock in the morning, but he won't over

talk me tonight. "Get that for me while I clean her up, Aleeaha," I said after hearing a knock at the door. I walked Saysha to the bathroom and turned on the water.

"Hey, Aunt Neicy," I heard Aleeaha say.

"Hey, baby. Where is Sabrina?" she asked.

"In the bathroom with Saysha.

I heard the front door close. "Mommy, who is 'dat?"I closed the bathroom door.

"Hold still," I said, wiping the grease off of her face with a wash cloth.

I took my time cleaning Saysha up because I wasn't ready to see my Aunt Neicy. Even though she is not actually blood related to my momma, they have been friends for as long as I can remember. I considered her family, too, and I wasn't ready to face any of them. There was a knock at the bathroom door.

"Who is it?" Saysha asked.

"Be quiet and turn around," I whispered in her ear.

"I got a twelve pack of Miller Draft, a two piece snack from Feather n' Fin, and nothing but time on my hands. I'll be out here waiting for you when you come out," Aunt Neicy hollered threw the bathroom door.

Aleeaha knocked on the bathroom door next and told me that she would clean Saysha up for me. Since I knew neither one of them was going to leave me alone until I came out the bathroom, I opened the door to let her in and went into the living with Aunt Neicy.

"You want a beer?" Aunt Neicy asked me, gnawing on a chicken wing.

"No . . ." I shook my head.

"I got some Vodka, too."

"I'll take some of that," I quickly said. That's exactly what I need right now, a stiff drink.

"You know how I do," she said, with food in her mouth passing me the bottle of Absolute Vodka. "Pour your own troubles."

I went into the kitchen and filled two red plastic cups with ice. "I only have some watermelon splash Juicy Juice to chase it with."

"Works for me," Aunt Neicy said, putting a French fry in her mouth. I started laughing to myself thinking about what Saysha said about Mj's French fry. I closed the refrigerator door, grabbed the cups, and passed one to Aunt Neicy. "Your momma is torn to pieces, Sabrina. You need to go see her," she said, closing up the chicken box, sitting it down on the floor next to her, and wiping her face and hands with a napkin.

"I'm not ready to do that, Aunt Neicy." I tasted my drink. "Mmmm . . . this is actually good."

"Sabrina, one thing you should know by your daddy's sudden passing is that life is too short. Folks is going away from here left and right and nobody is exempt. Look at Whitney Houston! I felt like somebody in my family died when I heard she passed away," she said, popping the top off a beer.

"Then er'body want to come out the woodwork talking about how much they loved and was going to miss her, but where were they at when she was alive?"

"Aunt Neicy, I don't mean no harm but what does that have to do with me and my momma?"

"No harm taken." She paused as she guzzled down her first beer. "Woo, that's good." She looked at the half empty bottle of beer. "And cold, too," She nodded her head. "Sabrina if something happens to Janis today they would have to pull you off the casket." She burped and then tapped her chest. "Umph . . . excuse me. The point I'm trying to make is when people are gone there ain't no second chance to do anything different. That's why they call the money you pay the funeral homes final expenses because there ain't no coming back or no do overs."

"Aunt Neicy, I am so tired of being lied to by everybody." I started blinking faster to keep the tears back that were about to fall from my eyes.

"I understand what you are saying. I've known Janis for over thirty-five years and I never knew that you didn't know that you were adopted until recently," she said, twisting the top off her second beer. "I don't know why Janis chose not to tell you. You will have to find that out from her, but regardless she is your momma and you are her child."

"How old was I when I was adopted, Aunt Neicy?"

"Sabrina, Janis was right there when you were pushed out the womb." She smiled.

"What do you mean?"

"Janis was visiting somebody in the hospital. Shit, I'm trying to think of who it was," she said, touching her forehead which indicated that she was thinking. "I don't remember!" She shook her head. "But Janis was getting off the elevator the same time as this pregnant woman was getting on. Janis said she was so petite in size that she was barely showing and she didn't know at first that the woman was in labor."

"The woman was pregnant with me?"

"Mmmm . . . hmmm," Aunt Neicy nodded. "And she was by herself. Janis helped her off the elevator and got a wheelchair for her. I guess they must have assumed she was family because they allowed her to go in the delivery room. After you were born Janis didn't want to leave the hospital until somebody came to see about her, but nobody ever showed up. She went back to the hospital the next day to check on her. You were still there but she wasn't."

"She left me?" My bottom lip started to quiver. *"How could she do that?"* I thought to myself. *"I could never do that to Saysha. What mother could?"* "Did she ever come back?" Aunt Neicy shook her head no and I could no longer fight the tears. "What about my father. Did he ever come to the hospital to see me?"

"No, Sabrina, he didn't."

I lowered my head and my tears were now landing on my lap. "Why would they leave me like that?" I covered my face and cried into my hands. "Why would they do that?" I started rocking back and forth. "What did I do?"

"Mommy, why you cryin'," Saysha suddenly asked.

"Take her in the room, Aleeaha," Aunt Neicy said, getting up and sitting beside me on the couch.

Saysha started crying when Aleeaha picked her up. "Put me down!" she kicked and screamed. "I want my mommy!" she protested. Aleeaha closed the bedroom door but I could still hear Saysha's cries. They matched mine.

"Sabrina, she was young." Aunt Neicy patted me on the back.

"It doesn't matter, Aunt Neicy!" I looked at her with my head tilted and whined. My nose was starting to run and I wiped it with my hand when I tasted it on my top lip. "I could never leave my baby like that." I yelled, pointing towards Saysha's bedroom.

"Sabrina you have always been surrounded by people that love you. Janis and your daddy raised you as their own and there was never a difference made between you and Stephanie."

I heard enough. I got up and walked to my bedroom as fast as I could, closed the door behind me, and locked it. I laid across the bed, buried my face in the pillow, and cried for people I never knew.

"*What did she look like? Do I look like her? Who named me? Do I have brothers and sisters? Did they ever go back to the hospital looking for me? Are they looking for me now? Was my daddy tall? Did they love me? Who am I?*" *These were all thoughts that ate at my brain.*

The Only Way to Strike Out!

My daddy may have only come around on the weekends but when he did come to see us he never came empty handed. He gave my momma money for the bills like clockwork, and even though we were poor we didn't know it because my daddy made sure we had everything we needed. He may have been cheating on his wife but he was good to my momma, and that is one thing I have tried to be for Sabrina. I know my daddy has rolled over in his grave many times looking down on me. I may have only been eleven when he died, but in those short years he made a huge impact on my life. There was one thing that he always told me, the only way to strike out is if you don't swing at all. Now it was my turn up to bat!

I went out the back door of Tonikia's apartment like I always did when I left her crib. I looked around to see if anybody was outside before I walked around the front of Sabrina's building to go in the house. I can understand the ladies not having faith in me, but you, too, fellas? I'm not fucking Tonikia contrary to what you may believe. I learned my lesson with Nicole, Asia, and Lisha. I will tell you about everything involving Tonikia later on, but right now I don't have a lot of time.

Surprisingly Sabrina was asleep and not up waiting for me to come in, but this is one night that I wish she was up so we could hurry up and get the fuck out of here. I turned the hall light on and went into Saysha's room first. When I picked her up out of the bed she started crying.

"Shhh . . . Daddy got you." I left out of her room and went across the hall to wake up Sabrina. "Bae," I shook her leg. "Sabrina?" I turned around and cut the light on in the room. "Sabrina, wake up. Shhh . . . stop crying Saysha."

"Turn that light off, Milk," Sabrina squinted her eyes.

"Bae, come on and get up." I told her, peeking out the bedroom window.

"Get up for what?" she hollered.

"I don't have time for that right now, Sabrina. Come on."

"Where are we going?" Sabrina sat up in the bed. "And where is Mj?"

"Sabrina, put yo' shoes on and let's go!" I peeked out the window again. "Hurry up!" I got Sabrina's purse off the dresser and handed it to her. "Come on, we going out the back door," I ordered her.

"Milk, what is going on? You're scaring me."

"Bae, come on. We don't have a lot of time." I followed Sabrina out the back door while still carrying Saysha. We quickly walked to the other side of Carriage House through the path that lead to the neighborhood Broad Meadow. "Go over to

that white van, Sabrina." I turned around to see if we were being followed.

"Milk, whose van is this?" Sabrina asked.

"Don't worry 'bout it, just get in." Sabrina got in the passenger seat. I passed Saysha to her and then walked around to the other side of the car to get in. I left the van running, so I put it in reverse and took off.

"Milk, what the hell is going on? Why do you have me and my baby out in the middle of the night like this? I have to go to work in the morning." She looked down at Saysha who had fallen back asleep.

"No you don't," I said. I looked in the rearview mirror and then changed lanes to get on the interstate.

"What do you mean no I don't?" She looked at me.

"Fuck that job." I looked at Sabrina and then back to the road.

"What do you mean fuck- Milk, take me back home." Sabrina sat up in the seat.

"That ain't yo' home no more," I told her.

"What the hell do . . ." She raised her voice and Saysha started crying in her sleep.

"You scaring my daughter. Just hold on we gon' talk."

Sabrina sat back in the seat and didn't say anything else to me until thirty minutes later when we pulled up in front of a four bedroom house.

"What are we doing here?" she asked, looking around.

"We living here for right now. Come on and get out of the car," I told her, going around the other side of the van to help her with Saysha.

"I'm not going inside of that house!" she protested.

"A'ight then, you can sleep outside in the van." I walked up to the front porch carrying Saysha in my arms. I unlocked the front door and took Saysha upstairs to the first bedroom on the left and then went back downstairs to deal with Sabrina.

"You just couldn't stay away from them could you?" she asked, looking around the house. She was still standing in the entrance to the front door.

"Stay away from what?" I asked even though I knew exactly what she was talking about.

"The streets!" she yelled. "I know damn well you're not house sitting!" I didn't respond. "You don't hear me talking to you?"

"I hear you . . ." I nodded my head. "Close the door, Sabrina."

"Well, answer me then." She slammed the front door shut and folded her arms across her chest.

"Sabrina, how long did you think we were going to live like that?"

"So what am I supposed to do just give my place up, forget I have a job, and go back to being a Virginia housewife like nothing ever happened?"

"If that's what you want to do."

"I don't believe you. So those years you have dangling over your head don't mean shit to you?"

"I didn't say that."

"I'm going home in the morning," she said, turning around and walking away.

"Come here, Sabrina," I called out to her. She walked up the stairs so I got up and went upstairs, too. Sabrina went into the room I put Saysha in and closed the door.

"Our room is down the hall," I hollered after opening the door.

"Milk, leave me alone."

"Come on out of here before you wake Saysha up." Sabrina didn't move so I went over to the bed, scooped her up in my arms, and left out the room. "I got something I want to show you." I said, while walking down the hall to the room I told her was ours.

"Milk, put me down."

"I was going to," I said, placing her down on the bed. I reached over and opened the top drawer of the night stand that was next to the bed, took out a ring box, and held it up in front of Sabrina. "Happy Birthday!"

"No, Milk," she said, moving my hand away.

"Whatchu' mean no? You ain't even look at it," I said, opening the box for her.

"I don't want it." She shook her head. I took the ring out of the box and took Sabrina's hand. "No Milk, I mean it."

"Look at me, Sabrina," I sat down on the bed next to her, but she stood up.

"I don't want to hear it, Milk."

"Bae, you got to hear me." I said, standing up, too.

"Milk, you promised me!" Sabrina lowered her head and started to cry.

"Sabrina, don't do that. Come here." I took her by the arm and pulled her close to me. "Sabrina, you have to let me be a man." I said, rubbing the back of her head. "I'm not saying that it's gon' be like this forever, but right now I have to do what I know how to do to take care of you and my kids."

"Milk, I don't believe anything you say. You're already back up to your old shit."

"What old shit, Sabrina?" I raised my voice.

"Bitches for one!" she yelled back. "I know you were with one when you didn't come home the other night until the next day."

"There you go Nancy Grace thinking you know every got damn thing!"

"I don't claim to know everything, but I know your black ass!"

"I'm out here trying to get above the poverty line, ain't nobody thinking 'bout no bitches."

"Milk, you didn't even try to. . ."

"Try to what?" I started yelling again. "Get a job?"

"Yes, get a job!" she yelled back.

"Sabrina, I'm a street nigga!" I matched her tone. "I have been taking care of my mothafuckin'

self since I was sixteen years old. I ain't never had to punch no time clock and I ain't gon' start now!"

Let's Rumble!

We have been having trouble at the club with the alarm system. The last time it was tripped the alarm company called Fox to find out if they needed to send the fire department. Fox told him yes and that he would meet them at Forbidden City. There was no fire when everyone arrived and it was a false alarm. Fox went to Dover Downs for the weekend, so when the alarm went off again tonight the security company called my phone. He had the contract set up so that if somebody didn't go to the club and manually enter the code they would dispatch the fire and police departments.

Any other night it would not have mattered to me but Onion should be on his way back with the dope. The last thing I needed were the boys in blue looking around and asking questions! I told the alarm company I would be there within thirty minutes, even though I knew it would take a little longer to get there. I'm on my way to Virginia from Charlotte, NC from an Executive Game. It wasn't business this time it was pleasure, but I had buzzard luck tonight. I almost lost the shirt off my back.

Tonight's game was sponsored by the Angreos Family. I know I should have gotten up when I lost all of my money, but the gambler in me wouldn't

allow me to do that. Plus I knew that we had a shipment of dope coming in tonight. By the time I put that work out on the street I will have enough money to pay the Angreos back, and after that I am going to fall back with the gambling for a while until I get my money back up.

I could hear the alarm still going off as I walked toward the club. The back door was still locked so somebody had to have gone out the side door causing the alarm to go off. Probably one of them bitches who danced. I punched in the alarm code and the noise instantly stopped. When I looked over at the front door I saw that there were two police officers waiting on the other side. "*Shit!*" I walked over to the club entrance to answer the door.

"How can I help you officers?" I asked, stepping outside the club so they would not come inside.

"Just patrolling the area and heard the alarm going off," the white officer stated, stretching his neck to look over my shoulder and inside the club.

"I think somebody may have gone out of the side door and tripped the alarm. I took a look around when I came in and everything looks to be in order," I answered. I started to sweat under my arms. After all, I did have five keys of dope in my office.

"We have time, it's better to be safe than sorry." He nodded his head at me.

"Actually I'm getting ready to lock the place down and leave myself. Thanks for stopping by and checking on the place. I'm sure my boss will really appreciate it."

"Alright. Have a good night." He tipped his hat at me.

"You too, officers," I nodded my head back and went back inside the club.

I went around to all the emergency exits to make sure they were pulled shut and locked. Everything was, including the back door I came in. I reached behind my back and got my gun. The only place I had not checked yet was my office.

"Yo, Onion," I called out. "You in here, man?" No answer.

I walked to the back of the club where the office was and it was locked, too. I dug into my pocket, got my keys, and unlocked the door. I reached my arm in and held up my gun. The room was dark and it didn't look like anyone was there. I slid my hand along the wall to feel for the light and turned it on.

"What the fuck?"

I aimed my gun at the body that was lying in a pool of blood faced down on the floor. I kicked the side of his leg and he didn't move. I looked around the room and the safe door was wide open. From where I was standing I could see that it was empty. I walked around to the front of the body and turned it over with my foot. I had to look away from him for a second. I have seen dead bodies before in my life time but looking at Onion's throat slashed along with the stab wounds on his face

turned my stomach. When I looked around the room the floor, chairs, mini-bar, and even Onion was doused in milk. That was Milk's way of letting me know that he was behind this.

Okay mothafucka', let's rumble!

Ward of the State!

"Milk, just take me and my baby back home," I said, walking towards the bedroom door.

"You can't go back to your crib right now it's hot, Sabrina!" I yelled.

"What did you do, Milk?" she asked, staring coldly at me.

"Don't worry 'bout that. This is where we are going to live for a minute so make yo' self at home.

"Milk, I don't want to be a part of that life anymore. I'm not going back to jail for you and anybody else."

"And I don't plan on it either, but I'm not going to be a ward of the state and neither are my kids. I don't need no damn food stamps and anything else they are offering to give you. I can take care of my own, and that includes you, too. Look, Sabrina, all I want to do is make you happy."

"Milk, what will make me happy is our family staying together. I don't want to put Saysha through anymore trauma. She may be young, but you don't know what kind of effect everything has had on her.

"Sabrina, you have to trust me. I love you and I love me, too, and the last thing I'm going to do is get caught out there again. I have a different set of

priorities now. It's not going to be like it was before. I promise you."

"I don't want to quit my job, Milk. I really enjoy what I am doing." I pointed out to him.

"Sabrina, why work for somebody else when you can have you own business." He lowered his head. "I really don't want you to work for real, but if you must, go into business for yourself.

"Milk, I don't want you to get hurt again," I softly said.

"Bae, nothing is going to happen to me. You have to trust me, Sabrina." He picked up the ring box that I had sat down on the bed and took out the ring. "I love you, Sabrina. Always have; always will." Milk slid the ring on my finger and even in the dim light I could see it sparkle from every angle.

"I love you, too." I reached up and kissed him.

Milk took off the shirt he was wearing and unfastened his button to his pants. Before I knew it they were around his ankles. Next he started to undress me. I laid back on the bed wearing nothing but the ring Milk had just placed on my finger and waited for him to join me. *'Why can't I ever say no to this man,'* I thought.

Milk skipped all of the foreplay and dove right in, but there was something different in the way he made love to me this time. He held me so tight there was little room for breathing. He had his arms wrapped tightly around me with both hands as he slowly moved in and out of me to the sounds of our heart beating. I closed my eyes and allowed the passion to take me away as I tightly put my arms around him and held on for dear life. Milk whispered in my ear several times that he loved me, and each time I told him that I loved him back knowing deep down in my heart that this would be the last time we ever made love.

After we had finished Milk told me that he had to leave out, not to call anybody, or tell them where we were. I saw him reaching up on the top shelf for something but I never got to see what it was because he tucked it in his back before I had a chance to see it, but I'm sure it was a gun. I was praying it would not have come to this, but Milk is on a rampage.

I waited until he pulled out of the driveway before I reached for my cell phone.

"Ma," I started crying. "I need you to come and pick me and Saysha up."

Run This Town!

I watched Yvette from the car as she walked into the middle building where I was parked in front of. I saw her walking out of the building shaking her head.

"Ain't nobody home," she said, closing the door behind her.

"How ain't nobody home? I see the light on in one of the rooms," I told her, growing angry at the fact that she may be lying to me to protect Sabrina.

My plan was to get Sabrina and her daughter out of the house and sit back and wait for Milk to come home, but so far my plan isn't going as planned. Thinking about all of the money I owed the Angreos family infuriated me, especially knowing Milk was behind it. If I don't get that money to them quick, fast, and in a hurry it won't matter how loyal Chino's grandfather was to my granddad. Money talks and bullshit runs a marathon!

I drove to the other side of Sabrina's apartment building. "Come on, we going around the back door." I put another clip in my gun and turned off the ignition.

"Rico, I'm not going to be a part of that. Yeah, I have done some fucked up shit to Sabrina because of you, but I'm not going inside her house with guns blazing and cause her or her baby to get hurt." I raised the gun to Yvette's head.

"Get out the mothafuckin' car right now!" Yvette opened the car door and tried to run, but she was no match for me. I caught up with her, put my hand over her mouth, and pointed the gun at her again. "Come on!" We walked over to the back door of Sabrina's apartment. I was all prepared to shatter the glass but I could see the door was slightly ajar. I made Yvette go in first, and then I followed her. It didn't take long to search the small apartment and it didn't look like anything was taken like clothes or etc. "You called Sabrina and told her I was coming didn't you?" I slapped Yvette across the face with my free hand.

"No, I swear I didn't. Sabrina isn't talking to me anyway. I don't know where she is. Please don't hurt me!" Yvette put her hand up to block her face.

"Bitch, I don't want to hear that shit. Now where is she?" I tucked my gun in my pocket and now had my hands around Yvette's neck trying to choke the life out of her.

Next thing I knew I was hit in the back of my head with something that felt like cold steel. I let go of Yvette, fell to the floor, and clutched the back of my neck. I felt myself being searched but I was still coherent.

"Get out of here, Yvette!" I recognized the voice and it was Milk. Yvette got up and ran as if her life dependent on it.

"I heard you was looking for me mothafucka'," he said, kicking me in my side. I reached in my pocket for the gun that was not there. "Looking for this?" Milk pointed my gun to my left temple. "Turn yo' punk ass over, nigga!" I didn't move so Milk turned me over with his foot. "New sheriff in town, huh?" He punched me in my face. "Mothafucka', I run this town!" Milk kicked me again.

"Fuck you, nigga!" I said, lying on my back.

"You know the last person who said that to me got his throat slit?" He started laughing. "So what you call yo' self doing, coming here to kill my whole family, nigga?" Milk pushed the gun up under my chin.

"Naw, motherfucka'; just you!" I was starting to breath heavy. He had my gun and I'm sure one of his own. I know he didn't come here to have a tea party. "Like you told me, whatever the fuck you gon' do, get on with it, mothafucka'!"

"Oh, trust me I am. Just not in here." Milk pulled me out the back door by my leg onto the ground.

When Milk let go of my leg, I used the other one to kick the gun out of his hand and it landed in the bushes. I got up as fast as I could to run over to the bushes to get it but I never made it to the bushes or my gun. The first bullet I felt hit me in my right leg. Milk must have had a silencer on his gun because it didn't make a loud sound.

"That was for my nigga Maine," he said. It was only a matter of seconds before I felt the next bullet hit me in my left thigh. "That was for Kirk," he said, walking up close to me.

"Uuurrrrgggg!" I moaned in pain. "What the fuck you mad, nigga?" I asked in between breathes. "You mad 'cause yo' bitch chose me?"

"That's what happens when you prey on the weak. Sabrina didn't know any better but when it was all said and done, who she come back to?" Milk bent down to get eye level with me. "I was her first and will always be her last."

When I saw Milk raise the gun up to my forehead I knew there wasn't nothing else for me to say. It was my time. I could have put it out there that I had been fucking Sabrina while he was locked up, but I knew she would be the third person Milk murdered today.

Images of my granddad and grandma appeared in my mind, but the vision that was there until the bullet left the chamber was Sabrina.

A Beautiful Disaster!

Onion is starting to become a waste of fucking time. I waited for him for almost three hours to come to the room and when he didn't answer any of my calls I left.

As I walked towards my front door I saw that the door had been kicked in and it was dark inside. I reached in my purse; got the gun Milk gave me a long time ago, and slowly went in.

"Oh, my God!" I jumped. "Milk, you scared me." I lowered my gun.

"You left my son in this mothafucka' by himself?" He walked over to me and stood directly in my face. I could tell by the flare of his nostrils that he was mad. I held on to my gun just in case I was going to need it. "You mean to tell me you couldn't sit yo' hot ass down for five minutes and take care of yo' son?"

"I was only gone for like twenty minutes and he usually sleeps through the night. . . "

"Bitch, you won't gone for no fucking' twenty minutes," Milk screamed. "I could hear him crying as I was walking to the front door."

"Milk, I-"

"Shut the fuck up! You just a piss poor ass excuse for a mother. I should choke the shit out yo' ass!" Milk had his fist balled up. I flinched, raised the gun up, and pointed it at Milk out of fear. "What the fuck you gon' do with that?" Milk snatched the gun out of my hand before I could react and he now had it pointed at me.

I started backing up. "Milk, I'm sorry!" I was starting to panic. "I really didn't mean to be gone this long."

"You damn sure is sorry. Sorry as a mothafucka'! You probably been leaving him in the house while I was locked up, too."

"No I haven't. This is the first time I ever left him in the house, Milk," I lied. "I swear!"

"Yeah, well you ain't ever got to worry about leaving him again. It will be a cold day in hell before you see my son again!"

"And what is that supposed to do, hurt me?" I started laughing. I no longer cared that he was pointing a gun in my face. "I could care less if I ever see you or him again with your broke ass. I was just waiting for you to come home so you could take him off of my hands, and feel free to take anything you may need out of his room." I sat down on the couch to eat the food I had picked up on my way home.

"Ain't shit to take!" Milk raised his voice. "The only thing you got in his room is a fucking crib. No toys, not shit on his walls, nothing. What the fuck kind of mother are you?"

"The last time I checked the only person who has to answer to you is Sabrina . . . so why don't

you go home and climb in bed with her and get out of my house?" I nodded at Mj, "and take dufus with you."

"Bitch, you lucky I don't beat women. You turned out to be a fucking beautiful disaster. Fuck you!"

Separate Ways!

I didn't go to Maine's funeral because I didn't have shit to put on, but I did see Tonikia at his wake. I thought for a minute that she was stalking me until my nigga Poochie told me that she was Kirk's younger sister. Shit, Kirk's pops was a rolling stone and he had kids spread out across Hampton Roads. With that being said, Tonikia was off limits to me out of respect for my nigga Kirk. Contrary to what you may believe ladies, niggas don't fuck just anything with a pulse or an eye in the middle of their forehead. We do have some boundaries.

Tonikia told me that she was going to Virginia State when Kirk passed away and he was paying for it. After he died—and after her second child—she ended up dropping out of school. I had to figure something out to get her out of Forbidden City plus take Byrd down, too, so she became my eyes and ears. I knew which days Byrd got his re-ups and how often he frequented the club. The first time I told Tonikia to set the alarm off I wanted to see how soon the fire department would respond. They were there in a matter of minutes.

Tonikia told me that Byrd usually took one of the dancers with him to meet up with the garbage truck that was coming down from New York, but he had something else to do and instead sent Onion.

That was my cue to move in. Tonikia set the alarm off when Onion went into Byrd's office with the dope. He came back out to deactivate the alarm, but when he walked back inside the office and closed the door I had my gun pointed in his face. He had the same scared look on his face as he did the night I whipped his ass for fucking up Yvette. Right after I slit his throat and left my calling card of pouring milk everywhere, Tonikia and I left the club tripping the alarm off again.

The nights I was coming out of her apartment we hadn't been in there fucking, I just stashed my gun in her apartment. Once I stole the dope and money Onion had on him, I stashed that in Tonikia's crib, too. I told her to see what she has to do to get back in school whether it is back at Virginia Sate or a community college. I owed that to Kirk.

The sun was about to come up and me and Mj were just getting home. I stopped and got Saysha some pancakes from McDonald's even though I knew I would hear Sabrina's mouth. She didn't like to feed the kids fast food.

When I got in the house, I put Mj in his high chair, broke apart a hash brown and a biscuit for him, and he went to work. I went upstairs to wake up his sister but she wasn't in her room. I figured she had gotten in the bed in the middle of the night with Sabrina like she always does, but when I went into our bedroom she wasn't there and neither was Sabrina. I looked around the room and there on top of the dresser was the ring I gave Sabrina sitting on top of a piece of paper.

"Milk,

The first time I ever laid eyes on you I was in love, and I must admit you swept me off my feet. For a while I felt as if I was living in a fairy tale and you were my knight in shining amour. Couldn't nobody tell me nothing about you that I wanted to hear because I was head over heels in love with me some Milton Woodhouse, but somewhere along the way I lost myself in you. Over the years the love I felt for you was replaced with resentment.

I blamed you for everything that was wrong in my life regardless of everything that was right. I have taken responsibility for the role I played in our sometimes dysfunctional relationship and you only did what I allowed you to do, so the blame not only lies with you, I'm just as much at fault. You may have been the one who was out in the streets, but the streets often found its way into our home.

Even though Saysha may not have understood what was going on the day she watched her mother and father be led away in handcuffs, I knew. As soon as I was able to hold my baby in my arms again I made a promise to her that I would never leave her again, and that is one promise I intend to keep. There is nothing I can do to change you but I can change me. A part of me will always love you Milk but deep down in my heart of hearts I

feel as if our relationship has run its course. It's time for us to go our separate ways.

I would never keep Saysha away from you because I know she loves her daddy very much, but I don't want you to come looking for me or start harassing my momma either. I will be in touch with you soon. Just give me some time.

Sabrina."

This Time!

It had been a month since I'd seen Milk and I needed to talk to him before I left town, if nothing more than for closure. He has not been calling me like he usually would do when I left him. He has bought me some clothes, shoes, and jewelry like he always does when he is trying to get back in good with me, but I gave it all back to him. However, I did keep the clothes and things that he bought for Saysha.

I told him I would meet him at Mt. Trashmore today so we could talk while Saysha played in Kids Cove. She was having such a good time that she didn't even notice Milk when he walked over to me.

"Thanks for meeting up with me." Milk said, sitting down on the park bench next to me.

"You're welcome."

"How you been?" Milk sat up, folded his hands together, and looked at me.

"I'm good." I smiled while nodding my head. "How is Mj?"

"He doing a'ight. I'm still taking him back and forth to the doctors right now. He is making some progress, but not much."

"Well, what are the doctors saying?" I asked genuinely concerned.

"One of the doctors at Kings Daughters says that he may be developmentally delayed, but he's sending me to a neurologist for a second opinion."

"How is Nicole handling all of this?" I asked out of courtesy.

"Nicole who," Milk sat back and rested both of his arms out across of the back of the bench. "I ain't seen Nicole since the last time I saw you. One thing you were right about, she don't care nothing about her son." Milk looked down.

"Who has been helping you out with Mj?"

"Besides Ms. Neicy nobody, but I can handle it. I ain't got no choice. If I don't who will?"

I looked at Milk shocked by the statement he had just made. That was the most mature thing I have heard him say in a long time. "Everything will be okay," I said, rubbing his thigh in a friendly way.

"Sabrina, what happened to us?" Milk asked, changing the subject.

"Too many things to name Milk," I said, moving my hand from his thigh before he got any ideas.

"Sabrina, regardless of everything I ever did I always loved you and I never put anybody before you. Ever! I don't think we had a bad life."

"We didn't have a bad life Milk because we have been living your life. I didn't have one. Everything about my so-called life revolved around you. Yeah, I did a lot of shopping and spending money unnecessarily, but what was all that for? I didn't go anywhere to wear the clothes. After everything that happened the clothes, the shoes, and the jewelry couldn't save me. I had no life. You were my life," I told him. "Worrying about who you were fucking this week or that week . . . that's what my life consisted of."

"Sabrina, a lot of what you used to accuse me of doing you was wrong about," Milk said sincerely.

"Maybe I was, but that's what I was led to believe by your actions. But Milk this really ain't even about the women."

"Whatchu' done moved on to somebody else already?" he asked with an annoyed look on his face.

"No," I calmly answered. "That's the last thing that is on my mind. My focus is on our daughter, finishing school, and doing well at my job."

"So you can't fit me in there no kind of way, huh?"

"Oh, there's plenty of room for you, but not everything else that comes along with being with you. I have accepted the fact that you are who you are." I saw that he was about to say something to interrupt me so I put my hand up. "Wait a minute and let me finish," I told him in a subtle tone. "I didn't come here today to argue with you. Really I didn't." I reassured him. I looked away from Milk to make sure I could still see Saysha and she was being followed up the slide by a little white boy. I turned back and looked at Milk who had a sad look

on his face. "Milk I gave you a choice, and you chose the streets."

"Sabrina, don't make it seem like I chose the streets over you and my baby. The street is what's taking care of you and my baby."

"That's where you are wrong at. The money you give to me for Saysha I give to my momma and it is being put into a trust fund for her. Sabrina is taking care of Sabrina and Saysha. If you see the streets as your only option there is nothing I can do about that to make you see any different, but I do have options when it comes to me. You have been shot, stabbed, beat up and sent to prison twice. People are getting crazier by the day and they are out here killing each other for sport. I am not taking any more chances with my life or Saysha's either."

"Sabrina, you know I would never let anything happen to you or my kids."

"I know you would just wake us up in the middle of the night to go in hiding. No," I shook my head, "I'm not going through any of that anymore."

"Sabrina, I'm not heavy into this shit like I was before. I just do enough to get by."

"Yeah, I can tell by looking at you that you do just enough to get by." I looked him up and down.

"Sabrina, don't act like I haven't spent any money on you and my kids. You the one who won't accept the shit I buy for you."

"Clothes, jewelry, cars, none of that stuff excite me anymore. Like I said, I may not have been out there in the streets with you, but I became just as addicted to the money and lavish lifestyle as you did and one day," I snapped my finger," it was all gone just like that."

"Bae, shit happens like that sometimes . . ."

"I know," I tilted my head to the side finishing the statement he was about to make. "It's a part of being in the game. That's what you were about to say right?" I raised my eyebrows for a response, and when he didn't say anything I kept talking. "That year when you were gone was harder for me than you will ever know. You never know how strong you are until being strong is the only choice you have."

"Sabrina, I was the one in prison. You think that shit was easy for me?"

"Milk, whether you realize it or not I was in prison right along with you. I think that is something you men don't understand. Bidding is not an easy thing to do and you try explaining to a two year old why her daddy can't come home when it's time to leave. I'm not putting her through that again."

"Sabrina, you are not going to have to! I just need some time to get some legit shit going and then I am gon' to fall back from all of this shit," he said, trying to convince me.

"Milk, you told me that six years ago when you opened up the fourth barbershop, so don't try and sell me no dream."

 Rayven Skyy

"So that's it?" Milk lowered his head. "You really gon' leave me for good this time?"

The Rumble!

Two years later. . .

The saying is if you love something let it go and if it comes back to you it's was always yours from the start and maybe that is true for some people but it wasn't the case for me. Any other time I would walk through fire if I had to, too get Sabrina back but not this time. I had to let her spread her wings and fly. If anybody in this world deserves a chance at happiness it was her. It ain't a broad out here that can fill her Gucci boots. I have to admit; a nigga was hurt for a long time after Sabrina left Virginia and moved to Atlanta.

Sabrina's daddy left her the house in Atlanta and she went back to school to finish her degree. Saysha is in school now too. I can imagine what the teachers are going through dealing with her. I keep her during Spring Break, the summer and Christmas break and you would think she was my momma instead of me being her father. Sabrina is doing a good job raising her too. She is quite the little lady and she can spend money just like her momma. I miss the hell out of both of them, but I had to get it together if nothing more than for Mj's sake.

His momma was wrong about him being mentally retarded, but he was diagnosed with Autism. I couldn't tell you were Nicole is or what she is doing. She was arrested for shoplifting in MacArthur Mall and once she did the ten days in jail that she was sentenced too I never heard from her again.

Yvette never bounced back from her drug use. She contracted Hepatitis C and died last year of liver failure. She never had a chance to make amends with Sabrina before she died, but Sabrina did come back to Virginia for her funeral.

Juju bought Cut N' Curl from Lea and is now a proud business owner. Him and Mike are still together and they just recently purchased a house out in the Church land area of Portsmouth. He was banned from competing in another Bonner Brothers hair show for flipping the judges table over after he had lost the competition for the fourth year in a row.

Ladybug, Sabrina's niece joined the Air Force after she graduated from high school and is stationed in Charlotte, North Carolina even though she had a baby in her junior year. Stephanie had custody of her daughter until she completed basic training. Ladybug met Dominique a month after she moved to North Carolina and six months later they got married at the Justice of the peace. I checked him out and he's cool.

Ms. Janis and Ms. Neicy are still thick as thieves and I don't know what I would do without them because they really help me out a lot with Mj despite the fact that Sabrina and I are no longer together. Ms. Janis and Sabrina were able to mend their relationship, but I can't say the same for her and Stephanie. I don't see any reconciliation with the two sisters anytime soon.

My brother Rell was finally released from prison after serving ten years in and he is already causing havoc in the streets.

As for me, I'm just taking all precautions to stay clear of the Feds. Since Byrd is no longer with us, I decided to take over Forbidden City in his honor and let me tell you, the shit that goes on in Forbidden City is worse than the shit you saw in the movie *The Players Club*!

You see, the rumble was never just out in the streets. The rumble is in our everyday lives whether you are rich or poor. Whether you hustle or work a nine to five. There is always a rumble going on in everybody's life, some people just refer to it as trials and tribulations or even a testimony and just like everybody else; I have one too. We all going through it because it's rough out here and the only thing we can do is do what we have to do to survive.

Well . . . I don't know what life has in store for me, but one thing I want to make sure is clear to some of y'all new niggas to the game. There are rules to this shit. Respect them. And to other hustlers in the surround states, you might want to think twice about coming to VA thinking you are

going to be able to feed off the land. Shit don't work like that around here as you can see. Stay in your lane, and we will stay in ours.

Once again it has been my pleasure speaking with all of you again. A nigga had it rough this go around, but I'm sure we will chop it up one day in the future. I know Rayven just has to introduce you to my brother. You think I'm bad? Shit, King Kong or Denzel ain't got shit on Rell!

In the meantime and between time . . . as always, be easy!

Bestseller!

(*Taps mic*)

Excuse me . . . is this thing on?

(*Taps mic again*)

Testing . . . testing . . . one two . . . three . . .

Oh, okay. Hey er'body, my name is Julius Wright known to some of you as Juju. Listen, I have been trying to get that jealous bitch Rayven Skyy to write a book about me. No, I don't do all that killing and I say no to drugs . . . unless it is a loud pack, but I think a book about yours truly would be a bestseller. Don't you? Good! I'm glad you agree. So here's what I need you to do.

When you post your reviews for The Final Rumble please mention the fact that you would love to read a book about me, and if you don't, I see Rayven is not the only jealous bitch out there! I would hate to have to shop my book around. I hear Cash Money is looking for some hot new stories and I would love to meet Wayne. I think we have a lot in common. So do what you can do to make that happen . . . okayyyy!

Smooches!

CPSIA information can be obtained
at www.ICGtesting.com
Printed in the USA
LVOW04s1511231115

463817LV00001B/71/P